THE TINSEL TAKEDOWN

❄

RUTH PENDLETON

CONTENTS

CHAPTER 1

❄

*L*izzy Thompson ordered cocoa at her favorite coffee shop, forcing herself to ask for an extra dollop of whipped cream to celebrate. Most days she used cocoa packets from the grocery store, heated up in a chipped mug at home, but today was special. She had just applied for a bank loan, which was a huge step on her path towards opening her own business.

She could get back to her frugal lifestyle after she celebrated. Right now, she intended to enjoy the ambiance, sitting at the small table she had managed to snag when the previous patrons left. With the pre-approval letter in her purse, Lizzy began to scan real estate listings for the perfect location, waiting for her name to be called.

The shop was crowded, with a line of people stretching back to the door by the time Lizzy's order was ready. She hopped up and headed for the counter to grab her cup, not even waiting to get back to her seat before she pulled off the lid to take a sip. As she did, she realized that the barista had forgotten the candy cane topping that was supposed to go with the peppermint cocoa. What was the point of celebration cocoa if they didn't make it right?

She turned in a slow circle with the lid off so she could show the barista what was wrong. As she turned back to get the candy cane, she collided with a solid figure standing behind her.

The cocoa went flying, emptying hot liquid in an arc across the floor before it rolled to a stop next to the chair leg of a very startled woman. Heat flooded Lizzy's cheeks as she tried to make sense of what had happened. The flush deepened when she registered that she had collided with a tall man in a blue dress shirt.

It took a split second to decide which problem to approach first. The man or the mess. She glanced past the man to apologize to the barista.

"I'm so sorry," she said, meeting the barista's amused eyes. "Do you have a mop or some towels I can use to clean this up?"

The woman shook her head. "We'll take care of it. Happens way more than you'd think."

Lizzy nodded, but she swayed on her feet, humiliated by the sight of dozens of eyes watching her. A tanned hand reached for her arm. It took a minute to register that the man she had collided with was holding onto her in an attempt to steady her.

With a sinking pit in her stomach, Lizzy realized that he was probably upset. Had she just spilled her cocoa on him? She looked at his chest, but his blue button-up shirt looked fine.

"Are you okay?" his voice asked. Somewhere in the back of her mind, Lizzy could tell he had an accent, but that thought fled as she looked up into his face.

The eyes that stared back at hers were so blue, Lizzy felt like she was looking at a painting of the ocean. He had wavy brown hair that he brushed to the side and light stubble across his jaw. Full lips parted in a small smirk.

A flicker of interest simmered beneath her humiliation. Didn't people always fall in love when they bumped into handsome strangers? That's how it happened in books, and yet Lizzy knew she wasn't living in a romance novel.

The man's smile dropped when Lizzy didn't answer. "Ma'am?" The pressure on her arm was reassuring. "Are you okay?"

She nodded. "I'm good. Thanks." The gentleman let go of her arm. As he dropped his hand to his side, she noticed a dark stain on the sleeve of his shirt. The collision with the cocoa hadn't been safe after all.

"I'm so sorry. Your poor shirt."

His eyes held a trace of amusement. "Are you sure you didn't do it on purpose? You wouldn't believe the number of times women have randomly spilled their drinks on me."

Lizzy wasn't sure if he was teasing her, but two could play that game. "Do you have a habit of sneaking up on unsuspecting cocoa drinkers? That might be part of the problem." She tried to hide her smirk.

"Only the beautiful ones," he said. "Can I buy you

another drink? I don't think you'll be wanting that one anymore." He jerked his chin towards the mess on the floor, his cheeks lifting to show a dimple. Of course, he had a dimple. It felt like the universe had opened a portal and transported Lizzy's ideal man straight to the coffee shop.

"You don't have to do that," she said. She was impressed she was forming coherent sentences at all.

"I know, but I'd like to." He held her gaze, and Lizzy's resistance melted. She wasn't looking for a boyfriend at the moment, but that didn't mean she couldn't accept a drink from a handsome man when it was offered to her.

"Thank you. It was a peppermint cocoa, with an extra dollop of whipped cream. I'm celebrating." As soon as the words were out of her mouth, Lizzy blushed. She wasn't the type of person who ordered extra anything, but this was a special day.

He raised an eyebrow but didn't say anything before he turned back to the barista to put in her order. The woman handed over a stack of napkins, which the man held to his sleeve.

Lizzy took the time to study the man, taking in his polished outfit, from the nicely pressed slacks to the European dress shoes on his feet. He clearly understood fashion, or he was coming off a photo shoot for a magazine. The look was somewhat ruined by the cocoa on his sleeve, which he was dabbing at with a napkin.

The man caught her staring when he turned back. His eyes gleamed, but he was too polite to comment. "It will be another minute," was all he said. Then he turned back to the counter, his voice low as he chatted with the barista.

Lizzy could hear her sister Maisy's voice in her head. *Get his number, Lizzy. Ask him out.*

She closed her eyes and counted silently to five. Someone starting up a business didn't have time for dating. It wasn't in the plan. College and career. Then marriage and kids. It didn't matter how handsome or charming the man in front of her was. She wasn't ready to start a relationship with anyone.

When he turned back to her, he was holding a new cup of cocoa. "Do you have a table or were you taking it to go?"

"I found a spot over there." She led the way to the table her jacket was sitting on before sinking into her seat. So much for taking the time to browse property listings. It would be polite to ask the man to join her.

"Do you want to sit down?"

The man's expression was difficult to read when he pulled out the chair. He glanced at his watch. "I'm on my way to an appointment, but I'd love to join you for a few minutes."

"That's why you look so nice." The words were out before Lizzy registered that he might think she was flirting.

"I beg your pardon?" His eyes crinkled with laughter. "Are you implying that I usually don't look put together?"

Lizzy laughed. "No. I'm honestly just relieved that I didn't spill cocoa all over the front of your dress shirt. The sleeve is bad enough."

"Let's just call it a happy accident. The meeting you part, of course. Not the cocoa part." He took a sip of his cocoa, a smile spreading across his face. "My friend told me to check out this shop, but I didn't believe it would be any different than the stuff I get at home."

His dimples were showing, a trait that Lizzy found incredibly endearing. "Where's home?" she asked.

Just as quickly as they appeared, the dimples vanished. "I grew up in Wisconsin."

He didn't say anything else, but Lizzy sensed there was far more to the story. She didn't want to pry. She sipped her cocoa while scrambling to think of another question. "You said you have an appointment soon. What do you do?"

That question brought the dimpled smile back. "I'm self-employed right now. I don't want to bore you with the details. You said you were celebrating today. Is it your birthday?"

It was Lizzy's turn to feel shy. Who celebrated taking out a loan at the bank?

"I'm working on a new project, and things are coming together. The cocoa was my reward for making progress."

"I see." He studied her over the top of his mug, and Lizzy's heart fluttered. She could stare into those gorgeous eyes all day. He opened his mouth as if to say something else, but then he took another long sip.

Lizzy knew her time with the man was limited. "If you're new to town, you should check out the shops on Main Street. There are a few city blocks filled with a variety of stores. Lots of tourists go there." She didn't tell him that her biggest dream was to own one of those stores.

"Do I look like a tourist?" He lifted his mouth into a crooked grin, and Lizzy could tell he was teasing her.

"Well, locals usually bundle up in sweaters instead of business casual, but you said you were on your way to an appointment. I guess we can let it slide this one time."

"I plan to stick around for a while, so I'll have to get to work on those sweaters. Have you lived here long?"

Lizzy nodded. "I grew up here. My parents moved after I graduated, but I stayed put. I'm attached to the mountains and the changing seasons. What about you? How long have you been in town?"

His smile fell. "Only a few weeks."

Once again, Lizzy could hear his reluctance to talk about home. She needed to steer the conversation in a different direction. "I'm glad you discovered this shop. Is there anything else you're looking forward to doing around town?"

The blush was rising on her cheeks again. Some people would construe her question as an invitation to ask her out, but that wasn't her intention.

A smile flickered across his face but then he glanced at his shirt. "I'd better get this cleaned up before the shirt is permanently ruined. Are you okay watching my cocoa for a minute while I head to the restroom?"

"For sure." Lizzy watched him walk away, her heart speeding up at the thought of him taking his shirt off to wash it properly. He looked amazing dressed up, but he'd probably look just as good wearing a casual t-shirt.

Her head was buried in her phone when he came back. The sleeve of his shirt was drenched, but it was dark blue now instead of brown.

"I'm pleased to report that your cocoa behaved properly the entire time you were gone."

His eyes crinkled. "That's a relief. I'm glad it wasn't an escape artist like your first cup." He reached for the cocoa but didn't take a seat.

Lizzy's chance to give him her number was slipping away. "Do you have to go to your appointment now?"

The man straightened the front of his shirt. "Regretfully, I do. How do I look?"

Lizzy studied him with an appraising eye. "You look . . ." Trailing off, Lizzy held back the words on the tip of her tongue. *Stunning. Perfect. Dreamy.* "Other than the wet sleeve, you look great. Hopefully your sleeve will dry out before your appointment starts."

"If not, it's okay. It was nice bumping into you." The man stretched out his hand, engulfing Lizzy's hand with his as he shook it. "I hope your day of celebrating continues to go well."

There was a brief hesitation before he let go, like he was going to say something else. Instead, he pulled out his cell phone.

The knot in Lizzy's chest loosened. He was going to ask for her number, and she wouldn't hesitate to give it to him. He was the type of person worth getting to know better.

Instead of pausing to ask for her number, he lifted the phone to his ear. "My appointment," he mouthed. "See you around." And with that, he was walking across the coffee shop, heading towards the open door.

Lizzy watched him leave, her mind whirling. She thought about running after him, but she hesitated for too long. She could see him through the window as he folded into an old car and drove away. In one small moment of hesitation, she had lost her chance. Now it was too late. She'd probably never see him again.

The celebration cocoa in her hands didn't feel so celebratory anymore.

CHAPTER 2

❄

*E*than Crandall's wet shirt sleeve tugged against his arm as he drove to his appointment. Most days, he'd be annoyed at the inconvenience of having his shirt ruined. Then again, this wasn't a regular day. He was about to sign the paperwork for his new business venture.

The woman at the coffee shop had been a welcome distraction. He had felt awful for her when her cocoa hit the ground, but she handled the situation with humor. Not everyone acted that way. It was refreshing to spend a few minutes with someone who could hold their temper.

Her heart shaped face and brown eyes kept him distracted on his drive. Every time he tried to focus on his maps or where he was headed, her smile crossed his mind. There were layers to the woman who had her light brown hair pulled up in a messy bun, but he didn't have nearly enough time to explore them. He hadn't even thought to ask her name.

That was a rookie move. The days of being afraid to ask a beautiful woman for her name and number were past him, but he still felt a flicker of doubt if she'd even be interested. She had seemed nice enough, but three weeks in the small town had taught him that most of the townspeople were friendly. It didn't mean anything.

Ethan had no doubt that as soon as his shop opened, he'd be getting to know a lot about the community. He hoped he could provide a service that the town would appreciate.

A short, red-brick building appeared over the crest of a hill. This was his destination. He turned off the map on his phone and climbed out of the car. There was nothing to be done to hide the wet spot on his sleeve, but hopefully the realtor wouldn't notice. Even if she did, she probably wouldn't say anything. She was about to get a big commission from him.

Signing the new lease papers took less than an hour. By the time he was finished, Ethan's hand was cramping from signature after signature, but his body felt buoyant. He had actually done it. In four weeks, he'd be the owner of one of the quaint shops on Main Street.

The woman at the coffee shop had mentioned visiting that street. He wondered how she'd feel if she knew he was going to be running one of the shops. Maybe she'd wander in one day, and he could remedy his oversight in not getting her information.

The thought of waiting a month to see her again made his stomach churn. He drove back by the coffee shop and went in, just in case she had lingered, but a quick glance in the direction of her table told him all he needed to know. The table now held a teenage couple, who held hands and gazed into each other's eyes.

As Ethan headed for home, he gave himself one minute to regret missed opportunities. There was no reason to dwell on an event he couldn't control. By the time he was pulling in front of his house, his spirits were back up. He was under contract for a store front. Now the hard work would begin.

* * *

A MONTH LATER, the wind outside blew briskly, making leaves skitter across the ground in shades of orange and yellow. Fall had officially arrived. Ethan stood outside his shop on Main Street, stomping his booted feet to keep warm. He had forgotten a scarf, but the excitement of the day was enough to keep him warm.

He was finally getting the keys to his shop. Gina Lincoln, his realtor, was due to arrive any minute, although she had the tendency to run late. Ethan used the time to study the other stores that fanned out on either side of his.

Each store featured a large picture window that jutted out towards the sidewalk, shaded with a colorful awning. The awning above Ethan's shop was striped with blue and white. Part of the contract Ethan signed was a commitment to retain the look of the historical street, which meant the windows and awning were to stay put, no matter how he remodeled the inside.

Ethan's face was pressed to the window when a woman's voice called out to him.

"You decided to do some window shopping after all," the woman said. It took just a moment for Ethan to register that this wasn't Gina's voice, and another to turn to see who was addressing him.

The warm brown eyes staring up at him sent a jolt through his body. He had given up any hope of ever running into the beautiful woman from the coffee shop, and yet here she was, standing on the street beside him.

"Something like that," Ethan said. He stretched out his hand, not wasting any time. "I didn't get a chance to introduce myself to you last month. I'm Ethan."

A smirk lifted the side of her cheek. "I'm Lizzy. It's nice to officially meet you."

Ethan's insides were jumping, like a butterfly had been set loose in his ribcage. He reached for his phone. "I wanted to get your number when we met."

"Even after I spilled my cocoa on your shirt?" She held the end of her scarf, wrapping the strands of yarn around her finger.

"Especially after you spilled your cocoa on me. Although, come to think of it, if you wanted to get my attention, there were better ways to do it."

Lizzy tilted her head appraisingly. "I don't know. It seemed pretty effective to me."

Ethan chuckled as he pulled out his phone. Gina

was going to arrive any minute, and he wanted to make sure he got Lizzy's number before they were interrupted.

"I'd love to take you out sometime. Maybe we can get cocoa, and not throw it around the store." He held up his phone. "Can I get your number?"

Lizzy tried to shake her head, but laughter bubbled out of her. "I'd like that."

A weight lifted off Ethan's shoulders once her contact info was saved in his phone. He had met several people in the town so far, but she was the one who lingered in his mind.

"Do you window shop around here often?" he asked.

"I'm actually meeting someone. My realtor." Her face lit up when she talked. "He was supposed to be here ten minutes ago."

Ethan's heart began to pound. "I'm meeting a realtor here, too." Pieces began to click into place. There had been two shops available when Ethan was looking, both across the street from each other.

"Did you buy the shop with the red and white striped awning across the street?"

Lizzy's face looked puzzled, but she nodded. "Yeah. I'm getting my keys today."

Ethan patted the window of his shop. "This one is mine."

The world seemed to slow as Ethan realized what that meant. He had regretted not getting Lizzy's number. Now he was going to see her every day. He wanted to jump in the air and kick his heels together, but he didn't want to scare her away.

"What are you —," Ethan started to ask, but his words were cut off by someone across the street.

He looked up to see Gina waving wildly. "Ethan," she was calling. "And are you Lizzy?"

Lizzy looked at Ethan with a confused expression. "I'm assuming you know this woman?"

"She's my realtor. I'm not sure why she knows your name, though."

Gina gestured for them to cross the street. "I'm sorry for coming late. Robert had a family emergency come up, and he asked me to fill in for him." She looked at Lizzy's face. "You are Lizzy Thompson, right?"

"Yes."

Ethan felt like he was watching a game that he didn't know the rules to. Sensing his confusion, Lizzy placed a hand on his arm.

"Robert was my realtor. I guess we are both working with the same firm."

Anticipation was building. If Ethan and Lizzy both opened shops at the same time, they were going to have so much to talk about. It would be good to have a friend to commiserate with.

Gina reached into her purse and pulled out two manilla envelopes, handing one to each person. "Here's your welcome packets. Make sure to read your letters from the mayor. He takes this historic street seriously. Especially when it comes to decorating for the holidays." She rummaged through her purse and pulled out two key rings, each with a small tag dangling from the ring.

"I know you guys have waited long enough. Let's get you into your shops."

Lizzy grabbed Ethan's arm, and a thrill shot through his body. He glanced down at her face, the excitement written across it matching his own jumbled nerves.

"Are you ready?" Ethan asked.

Lizzy nodded.

He pressed a hand to hers, and together they faced Gina.

"Alright. Who is opening the cookie shop?"

A jolt of energy shot through Ethan's body. "That's my shop," he said, just as Lizzy spoke over him.

"I am."

Ethan snapped his head to look at Lizzy. "I think you misunderstood her. She said the cookie shop."

"Exactly." Lizzy's hand dropped from his arm. "That's what I'm opening."

Ethan took a step away from her, the blood pounding in his head. He looked at Gina, trying to control his breathing. "I think there's some sort of a mistake."

Gina lifted the other keychain and read the tag. She held it out with a strained laugh. "This is a first. It says cookie shop too."

A trickle of ice ran down Ethan's spine as he tried to make sense of what was happening. He glanced down the street, looking for hidden cameras. This felt like an elaborate prank. Not real life.

Cars whooshed by, the sound of horns honking in the distance. All around him, the world continued to turn, but Ethan felt removed from his body. He held his hand out mechanically, reaching for both key rings.

"I guess we'd better see which key fits which shop."

He didn't have the energy to look at Lizzy's face. The betrayal and shock that had registered there moments before had been enough.

Moving mechanically, Ethan headed towards the store with the red and white striped awning. It was closer than his store. He held up the first key ring, but before he could insert it into the lock, a hand clamped down on his.

Startled, Ethan looked up to see Lizzy's face, a furious shade of red.

"My shop. My keys." Her hand jutted out in a straight line, waiting for him to drop them onto her palm.

Ethan held the first key ring out. Lizzy grabbed it and tried to turn the key in the lock. She frowned at him when it didn't turn and dropped it back to his hand with a huff. She grabbed the other ring.

No one looked surprised when the key easily turned. Gina let out a small cheer, oblivious to the tension that rolled off Lizzy in waves. Ethan wrapped his hand around his key chain, eager to cross the street to get away from Lizzy's accusing glares.

"Congrats," Gina said. Her face was beaming like she had just handed out an award. Ethan wasn't sure how she could be so oblivious to the situation unfolding before her.

"Thank you." Lizzy's voice was curt, like she was barely

keeping her emotions together. Ethan recognized that tone of voice. It was the same tone his sisters got when they were about to break down and cry.

"I'll see you around," he said. He stuffed his hands in his pockets and stepped to the edge of the sidewalk. A door slammed behind him, and Ethan flinched. Someone, somewhere, had made a big mistake and he and Lizzy were going to have to deal with the fall out.

Ethan had done his research before buying the store. There wasn't a cookie shop in the town. Now, thanks to some sort of paperwork snafu, this town was about to have two of them. He didn't know Lizzy well, but he was pretty sure she wasn't going to walk away from her dreams. Neither was he.

So much for running into the beautiful woman from the coffee shop. There would be no point in asking her out on a date, now. After the looks she had shot him, he was pretty sure she was never going to talk to him again.

He opened the door to his own shop with no fanfare. He held his head high while he walked to the back office. Then he slid down to the floor and buried his face in his hands. The excitement of getting the keys was overshadowed by the haunting look in Lizzy's eyes when she left.

That was going to be impossible to forget.

CHAPTER 3

❄

*L*ife threw curve balls at people every day. This was something Lizzy firmly believed in. As much as she tried to plan for those surprises, she was having a difficult time trying to wrap her mind around the complication named Ethan.

It felt as if the universe had looked inside her soul, created the perfect man for her, and then wrapped him in a package that would ensure they could never be together. There wasn't a future with someone who threatened to destroy her business before it ever had a chance to get off the ground.

Seeing Ethan get his keys was a shock that she still hadn't recovered from. It had been two weeks since they had bumped into each other on the street. And those two weeks had changed everything.

Every time Lizzy showed up to her shop to meet with her contractors, she couldn't stop her eyes from drifting to his side of the street. All too often, she'd catch a glimpse of his brown hair walking by, and her heart would skip a beat before she remembered that there was no reason for it to behave in such a manner.

She wasn't trying to spy on him. Not really. But she also wasn't trying very hard to avoid looking in the direction of his shop, multiple times a day.

Ethan had tried to reach out one time after they discovered that they were going to be competitors, but Lizzy didn't reply to his text. There was no point. She wasn't about to start a friendship with the guy who was standing between her and her dreams.

A loud clatter outside snapped Lizzy out of her thoughts. She ran to the back door and flung it open. Behind the shop there was a small parking lot that was mostly used by employees and store owners. A large delivery truck was parked outside with the truck door rolled up in the back.

Somehow, the driver had managed to squeeze into a small space between two cars. The clanging noise was the sound of a metal ramp that the driver was lowering to the ground. He walked up the ramp to the back of the truck and pulled out a hand dolly. While Lizzy watched, the man slid the prongs of the dolly between the slats of a wooden pallet, pumping the handle to lift the cargo.

Grunting loudly, the man tilted a large oven back and rolled it down the ramp, the top teetering back and forth like it was going to fall. The movement didn't seem to alarm the man, although he did reach out a hand to slow the swaying movement. Lizzy breathed out a tight breath, rolling her shoulders to try to release the tension in them when he reached level ground.

"I've got a delivery of two ovens. Where do you want them?" he asked, turning to face Lizzy.

Her mind was spinning. The delivery was a week earlier than she had expected. There wasn't even a place to put them in the kitchen, yet. The cabinets were still being installed.

Lizzy propped open the back door. "You can put them in the front of the shop."

The construction workers were going to have to work around the tall ovens for a few days until they could move them into place. Hopefully they wouldn't mind.

"Got it." The man wheeled the first oven down the skinny hallway, coming to a stop near the wall at the front of the shop. He raised an eyebrow as he scanned the room.

Everything was coated in a fine layer of sawdust. Even the spot Lizzy pointed to near the wall was covered. She reached for a broom, hastily sweeping out a large rectangle for the ovens to sit in.

"Sorry about the mess," she said. "I wasn't expecting the delivery yet."

He nodded. "Construction these days is always running behind. Throw a tarp over them and you should be good."

Lizzy followed the man back out, watching as he unloaded the second oven next to the first. She custom ordered them specifically for the shop. Each oven had metal rungs along the inside, made specifically to hold a dozen cookie sheets at one time. It certainly was going to beat trying to make cookies in her double oven at home.

"Thanks," Lizzy said.

The man handed over a slip of paper for her to sign before he climbed into his truck and rumbled down the street.

It took all of Lizzy's willpower to not tear off the plastic that surrounded the ovens once he was gone. All she wanted to do was take a peek, but she was pretty sure her customers wouldn't appreciate the taste of sawdust. Instead, she rummaged through her trunk until she found an old tarp.

"See you soon," she whispered to the ovens as she covered them.

She stood up, glancing around to see if anyone was paying attention to her. Most people didn't talk to the inanimate objects around them, but Lizzy did. She patted the top of the tarp and headed to the office to find her purse.

The first snowflakes of the season were dotting her windshield when she pulled out of the parking lot. Lizzy felt the whoosh of anticipation that came as the seasons changed. Fall would stick around for a few more weeks, but before long, she'd be fighting snowstorms on her way to work.

Lizzy drove to the outskirts of town where the local mill sat. She had learned early on in her baking career that freshly ground flour from The Old Red Mill tasted better than the stuff she could buy on the shelves at the local grocery store.

If everything went well, Lizzy would be opening in less than a month. She needed to set up orders with her favorite vendors. She had already gotten the dairy farm on board. Fresh milk would be delivered every week. Now it was time for the next staple.

She walked into the mill and looked around. A large desk sat in one corner, and shelves ran along two walls, filled with various types of flours. Lizzy knew that the magic happened behind the double doors at the back of the building, where the flour was ground daily.

"Hi, Kent," she said, approaching the desk. Kent looked up from his computer screen. His tousled blonde hair fell across his eyes, but he brushed it to the side and looked up at her.

A huge smile spread across his face. "How's my favorite baker?"

Lizzy couldn't help but smile back. "I'm working hard. The shop opens next month. I was hoping I could get a delivery schedule set up."

Kent nodded. "Zach is meeting with someone right now, but he should be done soon. He'll take care of you."

"Thanks." Lizzy wandered over to the shelves. She had been coming to the mill for so long, she remembered when it was owned by Zach's dad. Zach had taken over a few years ago. He was one of Lizzy's biggest supporters, ordering custom cookies from her for every special occasion.

A few minutes later, the rumble of voices came down the hall. The double doors swung open and the last person Lizzy expected to see walked through them. Ethan was laughing with Zach, his face bright with excitement.

"I can't wait to work with you," Ethan said.

Lizzy had a fraction of a second to look for somewhere to hide before she was spotted. She considered grabbing a bag of flour to pretend like she was reading it, but it wouldn't help. There was nothing in the open room to save her. She squared her shoulders and turned to face Ethan.

His face lit up when he saw her, and he walked to her side like they were old friends. "Hi, Lizzy. What are you doing here?"

The delicious scent of cinnamon mixed with a woodsy cologne clung to him as she studied his face. She had forgotten how good he looked up close. Glimpses through the window hadn't been enough. Lizzy could feel an involuntary quickening of her heartbeat just looking at the man.

"I could ask you the same thing. I've been coming here for years."

Something in the tone of her voice made him step back. "So, their reputation is as good as I've heard?"

Lizzy wanted to lie. This was her competition, after all. But she couldn't bring herself to do it.

"Yeah. They are the best."

His mouth twitched. "I'm glad." He shifted on his feet. "Uh, how is your shop doing?"

Lizzy blinked slowly. Was he oblivious enough to think she would share information with him? She didn't want his shop to fail, necessarily. She just wanted him to find a magic wand and transport his shop somewhere else.

"It's fine." Lizzy swallowed. The polite thing to do would be to ask him about his shop, but she didn't want to hear the answer. She couldn't bear it if everything was going perfectly for him.

She wanted a reason to hate the guy, but the blue eyes studying hers were sincere. He seemed like the person who would sit with her on the couch at the end of a long day, massaging her feet while she told him all her struggles. She couldn't let that guy get under her skin.

"How are things with you?" she finally asked, when the silence had stretched a little too long.

Ethan opened his mouth to answer but Zach cut in. "Sorry to interrupt, but I've only got a few minutes before I have to leave for my daughter's school play. Lizzy, did you want to get started?"

Relief poured through her body. She needed to get away from Ethan before she could fall any further under his spell.

"Yes, please." She gave Ethan a small wave. "It was nice seeing you."

"Take care, Lizzy." Ethan started to raise his hand like he was going to wave back, but he seemed to think better of it. He lowered his hand, rubbing it on his jeans. "Thanks again, Zach. I'll be in touch."

Lizzy followed Zach to his office, fighting the urge to glance back to see Ethan's face one more time. He was a complication she didn't need.

25

Zach gestured to a chair, inviting Lizzy to sit. As she did, she noticed the box sitting on a stack of papers near the edge of the desk. Her heart dropped. She'd recognize the shape of the box anywhere, even if there wasn't a sticker on the front that said *Ethan's Crumbs*.

"Did you know Ethan's opening a cookie shop, too?" Zach asked, following the direction of her eyes.

Her mouth twitched. "I've heard that."

"He brought me a sampler. Do you want to taste some?" Zach flipped open the lid, revealing four perfect cookies.

Lizzy's mind screamed at her to say no. Trying Ethan's cookies behind his back felt dishonest, somehow. Then again, he was the competition. It would be foolish to not learn everything she could about him.

She was spared the choice of answering when Zach broke off a piece of the chocolate chip cookie and handed it across the desk to her. Lizzy's hand shook slightly when she took the cookie, but she told herself it would be rude to say no.

The second the cookie hit her taste buds, Lizzy knew she was in trouble. The flavors exploding across her tongue were delicious. Her heart fell. She had been secretly harboring hope that Ethan's product would be bad. If her cookies were the best in town, he wouldn't have a chance.

Zach's eyes were closed. "Mmm." He opened his eyes and reached into the box. "I'm definitely a fan of the chocolate chip. Want to try the sugar cookie?"

Again, Lizzy was spared the chance to answer as Zach

held another piece of cookie towards her. Lizzy didn't hesitate this time but popped it quickly into her mouth.

She tried to be objective as she let the cookie dissolve on her tongue. There was a hint of flavoring that Lizzy couldn't identify. Like the chocolate chip cookie, it was absolutely delicious.

A cold band of fear gripped Lizzy's chest. Ethan was going to be real competition. He had the looks to charm the town and the flavor profile to back it up. It took all of Lizzy's strength to keep her voice calm while she set up paperwork for a recurring weekly delivery from the mill.

The tears didn't begin to fall until Lizzy made it to her car. She was sitting in the parking lot, trying to compose her nerves when a text from Ethan came through.

It was good bumping into you today. I'd love to catch up.

Lizzy dropped the phone like her hands were on fire. Even through the phone, Ethan oozed confidence. Was she really not even a little bit threatening to him? She turned the key in the ignition, heading for home.

Ethan would be waiting a long time if he wanted her to reply.

CHAPTER 4

❄

Getting the vendors in place was the easy part of opening the shop. The remodel was the part that Ethan was worried about. He was standing on a step ladder, a paint roller in one hand, when an elderly woman appeared outside his door. She rapped on the glass, giving a small wave.

Ethan set the roller in the paint tray and wiped his hands on his apron before opening the door. "Can I help you?" he asked.

"I'm Irma Mae, dear. Your next door neighbor." She held her hand out for Ethan to shake.

He took it gingerly, trying not to squeeze too hard. Irma had stark white hair that curled around her temples. Years of life had left her with wrinkles around her eyes and a frail body that looked like it could blow away in the wind.

"Which shop is yours?" Ethan asked, although he had a

pretty good guess.

"The quilt shop. Do you want to come and see?"

Ethan looked around his shop. He had a couple more hours of painting to do, and a list of tasks that needed to be addressed after that. There really wasn't time to be visiting neighboring shops. Ethan reminded himself that he was part of a community now. He could spare a few minutes to be friendly.

Walking into Irma's quilt shop felt like walking into an old home. Large quilts adorned every wall. Short shelves ran the perimeter of the room, each one crammed full of colorful bolts of fabric. Overflowing baskets were set at the end of each aisle. Ethan got close enough to one to read the label on the bags inside.

"What is a quilt kit?" he asked.

Irma Mae pointed to the quilts hanging on the wall. "Sometimes people need a little boost to get started on their projects. The kit has everything they need to make one of these quilts, from the instructions to the fabric."

"What a great idea." Ethan had only been in Irma Mae's shop for a few minutes, and he was already impressed.

"That's enough about me. Tell me a little bit about your shop. My grandsons say it's something to do with sugar."

Ethan grinned. "I'm opening a cookie shop."

Irma Mae held a wrinkled hand to her mouth. "Oh my. That will be wonderful. I want to hear all about it."

As Ethan spoke with Irma Mae, his jitters about opening the shop faded away. By the time he left her quilt store, he was itching to get back to the remodel. He was ready to be a part of the town's historic Main Street.

* * *

TWO WEEKS LATER, the shop had transformed. Ethan was waiting for the final delivery to finish off the kitchen. He stomped his feet on the ground, tamping down a thin layer of snow that covered the sidewalk. He was watching for the truck, which, unsurprisingly, was running late. Every day since getting the keys to his shop had been a grind, but he was finally almost finished with the remodel.

The shelving units that surrounded the main area of the store had been removed, making way for a long counter that separated a small seating area for customers from a larger work area where the cookies would be made. Customers would be able to watch as his employees frosted their cookies before handing them over.

A smaller room to the back had been plumbed to hold large sinks for washing and drying all the dishes they'd use each day. He had wanted an industrial dishwasher, but that wasn't in the budget yet.

Ever since he had realized that Lizzy was opening a cookie shop as well, he had felt a heaviness pressing down on his shoulders. He couldn't ask her to change her product, and he certainly wasn't going to change his. All he could do was make sure his cookies stood out from hers.

The competitive nature in Ethan made him determined to succeed, but it was difficult to stay amped up when the competition came in the form of the beautiful woman that made his heart stir. He wanted to take her out and kiss her upturned lips. Not drive her business into the ground.

Ethan checked his watch again. The delivery driver had texted that he was heading Ethan's way next, but the truck was nowhere to be seen. He was about to head back inside when he heard the growl of a large engine.

The truck turned onto the street and Ethan began to move the chairs he had set out to block off the parking in front of his store. He would rather inconvenience a couple of shoppers than have the truck block off an entire lane of traffic while they unloaded the ovens.

He was grateful for the space he had saved when the truck pulled to a stop. The driver rubbed a hand across his face when he climbed down. "I've got two ovens for you. Where do you want them?"

Ethan had finished the cabinetry on the wall the day before. "Right inside and to the left," he said. He watched as the driver unwrapped the first oven. It looked slightly different than the one Ethan remembered ordering, but he couldn't pinpoint why.

Together, they tried to push the oven into the space in the wall. The oven jutted out at an awkward angle instead of sliding into place.

Ethan realized why the ovens had looked different than he remembered. "These are the wrong ovens," he said. He could see his opening day going up in flames. He couldn't run the cookie shop without a way to bake the cookies.

The driver cocked his head to the side, studying the

space in the wall. "Are you sure? Maybe you measured something wrong."

Ethan shook his head. "I triple checked my work." He pulled up the receipt of his ovens on his phone. "Look at the front panel. My controls should be along the top. Not the side."

"Huh." The driver squinted his eyes. "Looks like you're right. Let me see what happened."

He went to the truck and came out a few minutes later, holding a ringed notebook. Ethan held his breath as the man flipped through the pages.

"That's strange," he said, slowing to a stop. "It looks like we already delivered those ovens last week."

Ethan pinched the bridge of his nose, trying to keep his voice level. "As you can clearly see, they aren't here. There must have been a mix up somewhere."

The man pointed to the book again. "The book doesn't lie. You're the cookie shop on Main Street, right?"

At his words, Ethan's stomach dropped to the floor. "I think I know what happened."

He walked out the front door, the delivery driver following behind. Ethan led him across the street to Lizzy's shop. He paused outside the front, straightening his shirt before he patted his hair into place.

It was a construction zone inside. A woman in goggles leaned over a power saw, the blade tearing through the wood. Ethan thought it was Lizzy until she looked up. She flipped off the saw and removed the goggles.

"Can I help you?" she asked.

"We're looking for Lizzy," Ethan said.

"She's in the back." The woman cupped a hand to her mouth. "Hey Liz. Some guys are here to see you."

Ethan brushed down the front of his shirt again, sucking in a quick breath when Lizzy walked out from the back office. She had her hair pulled back into a pony-tail, but strands had escaped and were curling around her ear.

"What can I do for you?" Lizzy's glance slid over Ethan to land on the driver.

"Did you get an oven delivery last week?" Ethan asked. It was a simple enough question, but a shadow crossed Lizzy's face.

"Maybe." She folded her arms across her chest, suddenly defensive. "Why? Do you need help picking out your ovens?"

Ethan gestured to the delivery man. "This guy just brought me the wrong appliances. I was thinking maybe they mixed our deliveries up."

She scrunched her nose up like she was considering her answer, but her arms fell to her sides. "That seems a little far-fetched to me, but you're welcome to check."

Lizzy headed to the wall and pulled back a tarp, sending a cloud of sawdust into the air. Ethan held his breath as he watched the sawdust falling to the plastic-wrapped appliances beneath. These were definitely his missing appliances.

He pinched the bridge of his nose again before raising his eyes to look at Lizzy's. "You put my ovens under a tarp?

In a construction zone?" It took every ounce of effort to keep his voice level.

"To be fair, I thought they were my ovens. At least I didn't put them outside." Her ponytail shook back and forth while she talked, but Ethan was seeing red. He wanted to shake some sense into her body. Did she know what sawdust could do to appliances?

Keeping his temper in check was almost impossible, but he turned to the driver. "Can you take care of this?"

"I'm on it."

Ethan nodded once and strode out of Lizzy's shop. He wasn't sure he had any nice words left in his body. If something had happened to the ovens while they were at her shop, he'd be stuck waiting for replacements. He was pretty sure she wasn't actively trying to sabotage his efforts to open on time, but it sure felt like she was.

A half hour later, the proper ovens were in place and Ethan's nerves were calming down. He was wiping down the counter when his phone dinged.

The text was short. Nothing more than a couple of words. But seeing the text brought on a new round of heart palpitations.

I'm sorry.

Lizzy was apologizing. The woman who refused to return any of his previous attempts to communicate had sent him a two-word apology. It wasn't a lot, but Ethan hoped it was the start of a friendlier relationship.

* * *

OCTOBER GAVE WAY TO NOVEMBER, and everything was falling into place for Ethan's grand opening. He spent his mornings training a handful of new employees, and his afternoons perfecting his recipes.

Ethan made up fliers to announce his grand opening. He paid Irma Mae's grandsons in cookies to stand on the corner, handing one to every person that passed. He left them to their business, watching the boy's faces as they waved the papers enthusiastically back and forth in the air.

He was on his way back to his shop when he saw Lizzy heading towards her store. She carried a large stack of boxes that was tilting precariously to the side.

He jogged to her side, getting there in time to open the door for her.

"Thanks, sir," Lizzy said. She lowered the boxes to the counter and turned to face Ethan, the smile on her face dropping when she registered who it was.

"Oh, hey." She stepped in front of the boxes, casually trying to hide them with her body.

Ethan held back an eye roll. "I got my delivery from Sally's last week. Their frosting dyes are the best."

Lizzy stepped to the side, flushing slightly. "Sorry. It's just, I'm not sure how I'm supposed to act around you. For all I know, you're trying to steal my company secrets."

The words were light, but there was an edge to her voice. Ethan shook his head. "If I was trying to steal your secrets, I wouldn't choose frosting colors as a place to start."

He looked around her shop. "I see you got your ovens in."

Another blush. "Yeah. I was worried the counters wouldn't get done in time. Thank goodness they did."

"I know how you feel. Speaking of which, I'd better get back to my shop." Ethan was still trying to perfect his grandma's molasses cookie recipe. He didn't have time for awkward conversation. Especially not with his opening day looming on the horizon.

Ethan headed across the street, his hands tucked into his pockets. He smiled when he passed Irma's grandsons. "How's it going?"

"Look how many we already gave away," Hayden said.

The stack was more than a third of the way gone. He gave the boys each a high five. "You guys are doing great. Thanks."

A half hour later, Ethan was sliding a new batch of cookies into the oven. He had made what he hoped would be the last tweak to the recipe. He was washing the mixing bowl in the kitchen when a loud bang on the door made him jump.

The boys were probably ready for their cookies. He dried his hands on a towel and headed for the door, surprised to see Lizzy standing there instead. Her shoulders were hunched over in the cold. Ethan unlocked the door, opening it wide.

"Did you think I wouldn't notice?" she asked, pushing her way into the store. Her eyes glared at him with such anger, he took a step back.

"Uh, I'm not sure?" He wasn't sure where the line of questioning was coming from, or what he'd done to deserve her wrath. "What's going on?"

Lizzy's face turned a deep shade of red. "Why did you hand out those fliers?"

Confusion swirled through Ethan's mind. As far as he knew, advertising was allowed on street corners. So was handing out fliers. Maybe he had missed another one of the mayor's unusual rules.

"I'm sorry if the boys handed you a flier. I didn't think to ask them to skip your shop." He folded his arms across his chest, feeling attacked for no reason.

Anger was rolling off Lizzy in waves. She held up a bright red paper. "You think I'm upset because I was handed a flier?"

Ethan had a feeling there wasn't a safe way to answer that question. "Well, that is what you are waving in front of me, isn't it?" He smiled, making sure she could see his dimple. Women had told him more than once that his crooked smile was disarming. If ever there was a situation that needed some charm, this was it.

Lizzy slammed the flier down on the counter and jabbed her finger at it. "Were you trying to be funny or were you intentionally trying to sabotage my opening day?"

Ethan scanned the flier. Everything looked like it should. He had the name of his shop, the cookie flavors that were coming, and the opening date. Was she angry that they both had similar cookies on their menu? There were only so many of the classic flavors to work with.

"You're going to have to help me out here. What did I do?" Ethan didn't have time to sit around arguing but he was pretty sure she wouldn't want to skip to the kiss-and-make-up part of the argument either.

"You really don't see anything wrong with this?" Lizzy asked. "Look closer."

She pointed to the shop's opening date. As Ethan followed her finger, his body froze. The date was there, in large numbers. Somehow, despite all his careful checking, he had managed to mistype the most important part of the flier.

It was the day a cookie shop was opening. It just wasn't the right date for his shop.

He had messed up, alright, and the expression on Lizzy's face told him he wouldn't be able to fix it. So much for trying to win over the woman across the street. He'd be lucky if she ever spoke to him again.

CHAPTER 5

❄

*L*izzy was beginning to understand the phrase "wind taken out of their sails." The dream of opening her own shop was edging closer and closer to a nightmare with every setback possible. Seeing Ethan's fliers was the final straw.

She called her sister, ready to quit on the spot. "Maisy, I swear, the universe is throwing everything possible in my path. Maybe I should quit now before I sink any more money into a failing venture."

As usual, Maisy was her upbeat self. "What do we say about failure?"

If reaching through the phone to throttle her sister was an option, Lizzy would have taken it. Instead, she took a deep breath and recited back the words. "You automatically fail if you don't try."

"Exactly."

"But Maisy, this isn't something like studying harder to

ace a difficult test. I can do everything right and still fail miserably."

Maisy started humming in the background.

"Are you even listening?" Lizzy asked.

The humming stopped. "Sorry. I was trying to think of something comforting to say. All I've got is that I believe in you. I've seen you come up with solutions that the rest of the world would never have imagined. You're at the hardest part of opening your shop. Don't let a little setback drag you down."

Lizzy grimaced, glad her sister couldn't see her expression. "Thanks." Her sister was trying to be supportive, but she didn't understand what Lizzy was going through or how difficult it was to be trying to start her own business. Very few people could relate to that.

Dreamy blue eyes flickered through her mind, and Lizzy's fists involuntarily balled up. Ethan understood how hard this would be. That was probably why he was trying to sabotage her. He had seemed so genuine though. It was difficult to believe he'd be that conniving.

Lizzy sank to the ground, hidden by the cookie counter. She buried her face in her hands and held back a scream. Ethan had taken her final piece of control by messing up the fliers. He had apologized profusely, but it didn't matter. In a week, people were going to be lining up outside his cookie shop instead of hers. She was already starting the game in second place because people would go to his shop first before making their way to hers.

Second place. An afterthought. The person you went to if the main shop wasn't open. It wasn't acceptable.

She hadn't tried to edge him out for the first grand opening date. The fact that it had worked out that way had been a blessing that was now completely ruined. Lizzy could sit on the floor in a puddle of tears, or she could figure out a way to turn things around.

There was an order of custom sugar cookies waiting for Lizzy's attention. The bride-to-be was getting married in a month. Her bridesmaids wanted to serve heart shaped cookies with the wedding rings on them at the shower.

That gave Lizzy an idea.

The next few days she turned her anger into frantic energy. Her employees looked at her like she was crazy when she told them the amount of cookies she wanted them to make.

"That's more cookies than we have people in this town," Maria said.

"Not quite, but I want to make sure we have enough cookies for everyone." Lizzy piped a thin line of frosting around the sugar cookie, filling it in with blue frosting.

The day before the shop opened, Lizzy called in favors from all her friends. "It's time to make our mark," she said. She handed each person a basket filled with cookies. "I want to make sure every single person you can find will know about our shop opening in the morning."

"You mean everyone but Ethan's Crumbs, right?" Kitty asked.

Lizzy grinned. "I especially want Ethan to know that we

are opening tomorrow. He tried to steal our customers, but that isn't going to work."

Maria started laughing. "I get it now." She held up a cellophane bag which had been tied with curly ribbon. Inside the bag was a sugar cookie shaped like a blue ribbon with #1 piped in the center.

"Our customers should know that this shop is number one today, tomorrow, and hopefully every other time they want a cookie."

Giving away free cookies the day before the grand opening with a coupon for a second free cookie the following day was a risky move, but it was something Lizzy was willing to do if it helped her to build up loyal followers. She expected to lose money in the beginning but hoped she'd be able to recoup the costs later.

She wished she could see the expression on Ethan's face when he got her special cookie delivery. Her workers left the store, and Lizzy got to work arranging supplies under the counter. She was triple checking that they had enough boxes to keep up with the large number of orders she hoped to get when the bell over the door chimed.

Ethan paused in the doorway, brushing snowflakes off his coat before he stepped all the way in. Lizzy attributed the flutter in her stomach to the fact that he was coming to yell at her. It had nothing to do with the way the cold brought out a flush in his cheeks which somehow looked endearing on him.

The flutter definitely had nothing to do with the

crooked smile he gave her as he stayed planted on the welcome mat. "May I come in?" he asked.

"You already are," Lizzy pointed out. She silently lectured the butterflies in her stomach to be still. He was the one in the wrong here.

"I'm checking to see if there's anything I can do to help with your grand opening tomorrow."

"Why would you do that?" Lizzy's mind was searching for the trap.

Ethan ran a hand through his hair. "I know I've apologized for the flier mix up, but I really do feel bad. I want to make sure you're going to be able to open without my fliers messing you up."

The words were kind, but Lizzy could detect a hint of condescension in his tone. "You don't think I can open on my own?"

That cleared the smile off Ethan's face. "I didn't say that."

"I think we have things managed here just fine, but thanks for asking." Lizzy was guessing he hadn't seen her cookies yet. She turned back to the cookie boxes she had started to assemble, but the door didn't chime again.

"Do you need something else?" Lizzy asked. She kept her eyes focused on the box in front of her. If she didn't turn around, then she wouldn't have to stare at Ethan's handsome face. It was a distraction that she didn't want or need.

Ethan cleared his throat. "I." He paused, clearing his

throat again. "I know we're competitors and all, but can we call a truce?"

Lizzy spun around to face him. "Why would we do that?"

Ethan walked to the counter and leaned against it. He was close enough for Lizzy to smell that intoxicating cologne again, but this time the hint of cinnamon was gone. It had been replaced by molasses. His eyes were bright when he spoke.

"I thought I was lucky for bumping into you at the coffee shop that day. It felt like we had a chance at being friends before we realized we were going to be competitors. Why should that change just because we both like baking?"

Lizzy opened her mouth to retort, but snapped it shut when she noticed the edge of a cellophane bag sticking out of his pocket. He had gotten her cookie delivery after all, along with the not-so-subtle message that she had the best cookie shop in town.

"Did you like my delivery?" she asked, batting her eyelashes. She wouldn't tell him that she had wanted a friendship, too. Not with her opening day on the line.

Ethan flinched back before he turned his crooked smile on her. He headed for the door, pausing to look back. "I guess we'll see what our customers have to say when the dust settles. Good luck with your opening day."

He left the shop, taking Lizzy's spunk with him. Where was the fun in sparring if only one party was willing to play? She closed her eyes and ran through her checklist one more time before admitting that she was as ready as she was going to be. In less than twelve hours, the shop would be up and running.

* * *

THERE WAS something sitting in the doorway when Lizzy arrived at the shop the next morning at 4:30 a.m. As she got closer, she could see that it was a vase filled with yellow roses, a note nestled between the leaves.

Good luck with your opening day. I genuinely hope it goes well. - Ethan

Lizzy glanced over her shoulder at Ethan's shop, but the lights were still out. That meant he either made the delivery late last night or he had gone back home to get another couple hours of sleep. Either way, it didn't matter. Since he wasn't around, she lifted the flowers to her face, inhaling deeply.

"Thanks, Ethan," she whispered to the wind. It was a kind gesture, but Lizzy couldn't allow herself time to think about that. She had way too much work to do.

A half hour later her employees showed up. Between the four of them, she hoped they'd be able to keep up with the customer demand. She wanted to hire another person, but she couldn't justify the cost.

Customers were lining up outside the shop by six, bundled in heavy coats and scarves, vying for the chance to win a ycar's worth of cookies. The potential to win had been a better incentive than she expected.

At 7:15 she noticed a disturbance outside. Her future customers were turning their faces away from the store, looking in a different direction. She didn't care what was pulling their attention until the first person stepped out of line, turning to walk away. A couple of minutes later, the customer was back, this time holding an insulated paper cup that he sipped from.

He must have gotten something from the coffee shop down the street. It didn't matter what he was doing though. Lizzy put her head down and got to work pulling another tray of cookies out of the oven. They were running out of places to put the trays, which meant that they needed to switch gears.

"Frosting time," Lizzy called, pulling out a bucket of powdered sugar.

Maria looked up from where she was mixing. "Where are all these people getting their drinks from? I don't recognize the cups."

Lizzy had stopped paying attention to the line. She glanced out the window and waved at everyone to hide the fact that she was spying to see what was happening. Sure enough, dozens of people were now holding small red insulated cups.

As she watched, she could see people with bright red hats bobbing back and forth through the line as they handed the drinks out. The reaction every time was the same. The person would take a cup, smile, and then turn to look at Ethan's shop.

A pit gaped open in her stomach. Ethan wouldn't stoop

so low as to advertise his own business on her opening day, would he?

Lizzy decided to ignore the shenanigans of the line outside. She was supposed to be opening the doors in a half hour, and she wanted to be ready for the rush that was waiting to enter.

Ten minutes before it was time to open, Lizzy called her employees to her cramped office.

"Thanks for all your help this morning guys. I know it's early, and we've already been on our feet for hours, but hopefully our hard work will be paying off soon."

"What if we run out of something?" Maria asked.

"I honestly hope we do," Lizzy said. "If we run out, offer a different selection and then encourage the customer to come back tomorrow, when we'll be restocked."

Robert was re-tying his apron. "Won't that make people mad?"

"It is our grand opening. I'm pretty sure the customers will be a little more understanding than on normal days."

Robert nodded. "I hope so, too."

"Are you guys ready to make a lot of people happy?" Lizzy asked.

Maria, Robert, and Lisa nodded.

"Alright. Let's do this." The excitement was palpable as Lizzy walked to the door, turning the deadbolt before she flipped the sign in the window to open.

It was surreal watching the customers file in, with so many people waiting outside that they couldn't all fit in the shop. Lizzy handed out her grand prize coupons to the first twenty customers, telling them they'd won a free cookie every month for an entire year. One woman was so excited, she burst into tears while she jumped up and down.

The next ten customers won one free cookie each week for a month. Lizzy's heart lifted when she saw how excited each one of them was. Her hope was that they'd turn into regular customers. The bin for the grand prize drawing was rapidly filling.

Lizzy was working the register when she got a good look at one of the red cups that a customer left behind. It took all her willpower not to march out the door and wave the cup in Ethan's face.

He had apologized for the date mix-up. He had wished her well. Lizzy had even started to believe he was a genuine person, but the sticker on the insulated red cup made her question if he had ever been honest with her.

The name emblazoned across the front made it very clear that Ethan was playing games. The sticker simply read:

Ethan's Crumbs

CHAPTER 6

❄

*H*anding out cocoa had been a flash of genius for Ethan. He knew, because of the flier mix up, that people would be lining up outside his shop on the wrong day. The last thing he needed was people hating him because of a mistake.

Adding the stickers to the cup was a calculated risk. Lizzy wasn't going to like it, but they were, in fact, competing for the same customers. He figured the stickers were subtle enough, Lizzy wouldn't even notice.

From the looks of things, her shop had been busy all day. Ethan was happy for her. He pushed the small voice out of his head that told him she'd already won all the customers and tried, instead, to focus on his last-minute tasks before his own shop opened the next morning.

Ethan was hanging his spatulas on a hook when there was a knock on the glass door. A very persistent, angry knock that left Ethan with no question as to who he would see when he turned around. Sure enough, Lizzy stood outside the door, hands on her hips, with a look in her eyes that made him swallow a few times before unlocking the door.

"Do you think you are funny?" she asked, pushing her way past Ethan to stand next to his counter.

"I mean, yeah. A little. My friends usually laugh at my sarcasm." He was dodging the question.

Lizzy's eyes narrowed further. She took a step towards him, her finger out. "The cocoa? You couldn't just let me open my shop without interfering, could you?"

Ethan gulped. "I knew people would be showing up here because of the flier mistake."

"The intentional flier debacle," Lizzy hissed.

"The accidental, purely coincidental, not-on-purpose-at-all flier mistake." Ethan paused to take a breath. "You have to believe me. Mixing up the dates was a genuine mistake."

"Fine. But handing out branded cocoa cups was not."

She had him there. "You're right. I thought I'd send people to your line with a smile on their face instead of them being upset. From what I could see, it worked. You were busy all day."

Lizzy sniffed; her nose high in the air. "I would have done just as well without the cocoa."

"That is true. I'm sorry." Ethan held out a cookie. "Can I send you on your way with a peace offering? Just so you remember that I'm not a bad guy?"

Lizzy took the cookie, holding it between her fingers

like it was poisonous. "Look. I wanted to think we could be friends, but our shops put us in direct competition with each other. Things would feel different if you had opened a shoe shop."

"Yeah. But shoes don't taste as good." He held her gaze, waiting for a crack to open. After a moment, Lizzy began to smile.

"You've got a point." She raised the cookie to her nose, inhaling deeply before she took a small nibble. Her eyebrows lifted briefly, then she closed her eyes, chewing slowly.

He was holding his breath when Lizzy opened her eyes. "Molasses?" she asked.

Ethan nodded.

"And a hint of cloves?"

"Not quite. Are you trying to steal my recipe?" Ethan was joking, but a scowl flashed across Lizzy's face.

"I wouldn't do that. I have my own recipes."

"It was a joke." Ethan rested his hand on Lizzy's arm. "I really would like it if we could at least be cordial when we bump into each other on the street."

The scowl on her face twitched, and then she gave a wry smile. "I can try. Although, if you pull another stunt like you did with the cocoa, all bets are off."

Ethan waited until the shop door closed behind Lizzy. Then he got back to work. His nerves were a jumbled mess when he left the shop for the evening, but he was ready. The doors to Ethan's Crumbs were opening in the morning. He hoped the town still wanted treats after Lizzy's grand opening.

* * *

OMINOUS, gray clouds hung low in the sky when Ethan arrived at the shop the next day. He had planned for everything, except for the blizzard that began to dump snow two hours before he was supposed to open. Every time he glanced out the window, another inch of snow had been added to the ground.

Chad joked that they were going to have to spend the night there, asking if Ethan had thought ahead to provide sleeping bags for his employees.

Kitty looked up from the frosting she was mixing. "I live right around the corner. We can tape some boxes to our feet and snowshoe our way to my house. You guys will have to fight over the couch though."

The snow shifted from large, billowing flakes to sharp, icy pellets that banged against the windows. An hour before the shop was supposed to open, Ethan began to get worried. People had been lining up by this time the previous day for Lizzy's grand opening. Between the snow and the town's already full bellies, Ethan was beginning to wonder if he was going to get any customers at all.

A snowplow roared down the street, spraying a sheet of ice against Ethan's windows. Even if the blizzard stopped, there was nowhere for the cars to park. The snowbanks were growing higher and higher with each pass of the snow plow.

A half hour before opening, Ethan started to calculate the costs of how many cookies he was going to have to donate. The local food bank would take them, but they didn't pay. He hoped he could survive the pinch of his opening day.

Ten minutes before the store was supposed to open, the storm picked up so that snowflakes were sheeting down out of the sky, covering the sidewalk as soon as Chad passed over it with a shovel. Ethan watched his employee struggling in the bitter wind, and he made a snap decision. He called Chad to come in.

"I'm sorry, guys. It looks like we're going to have to postpone the grand opening until the weather clears up."

Kitty's face fell. "But what about all the cookies?"

That was a gut punch to Ethan. "I hate to see them all go to waste, but I'm not sure what else we can do. The weather isn't exactly clearing up."

"Are you sure?" Chad's brow furrowed. "I can stay."

Ethan realized that getting his employees home was going to be a concern. He sent a quick text to Sarah and Kim, telling them not to come in at all. There was already four inches of snow on the ground, with more falling. "You guys are welcome to hunker down here as long as you'd like. I'm sure the snow will let up eventually."

As he spoke, the lights in the store flickered once before shutting off. A power outage was the last thing Ethan needed. He looked out the window to see if any of the other shops around him were experiencing the same thing. All the shops across the street still had power. He opened the door and peered up and down his side of the street. Every shop window was dark.

"Alright. That's the final straw." Ethan pulled out his phone and studied the weather report. According to the app, there was supposed to be another five inches of snow over the next couple of days. He grabbed a marker and wrote a sign that he hung in the window. *Grand opening delayed until November 18.*

He had planned for a number of opening-day scenarios, but he hadn't planned for a blizzard that was completely out of his control. It wasn't going to be easy to make up those missing profits, but Ethan wasn't ready to give up.

Chad and Kitty looked up at him. "What are we supposed to do now?" Kitty was trying to be brave but the quaver in her voice betrayed her unease.

"I don't know."

With the power out, the heater was no longer working. In this kind of weather, the temperatures were going to drop rapidly until the inside of the shop felt more like a freezer than a store.

"Do you guys think you can get home?" Just asking the question made Ethan's stomach sick. He wasn't eager to send two young adults into a storm like this. Between the snow cascading down outside and the power being out inside, Ethan was stuck with no good options.

Chad nodded, but Kitty shook her head. "It isn't safe for you to drive, Chad."

"My parents put new snow tires on the jeep last week. I'll be okay getting home. I can take you, too, so you don't have to walk." Chad looked at Kitty to see what her answer would be.

"That would be nice."

Ethan's stomach was tying in knots. He wasn't a parent, but he knew he wouldn't send his own kid out in this kind of a storm.

"What if you wait a little longer for the snow to at least slow down a little bit?" Ethan asked.

It was Kitty's turn to nod in agreement while Chad shook his head. "Look at the sky. I don't see the snow letting up any time soon. We're better off dealing with this before the roads ice over."

He had a point. Ethan locked the front door and headed to the back where Chad's jeep was parked. It took all three of them working together to get the windshield cleared off. By the time the rest of the windows were clear, the front windshield was covered in a light dusting of snow again.

"Are you sure about this?" Ethan asked.

Chad nodded. "We'll be fine. This isn't my first time driving in snow."

"Okay. Text me when you're home so I know you made it safe."

"Will do." Chad climbed into the jeep and turned the engine on, the windshield wipers shuddering before they began to rhythmically clear the window.

Kitty gave a small wave and a smile before she buckled her seatbelt.

Ethan stood in the doorway, holding his breath as Chad fishtailed in the parking lot for a moment before the tires caught. He glanced at the time on his watch. If he hadn't heard from them in a half hour, he would check in.

With his employees gone, there was nothing else to do but head back inside. Even with the power out, Ethan still had a lot of cleaning up to do. The trays of cookies that were waiting for customers were going to have to be packaged up. He wasn't excited to do that by the dim light streaming in from the windows, but he didn't really have a choice.

Ethan was setting a large box of oatmeal chocolate chip cookies on a shelf in the back when there was a loud banging at the door. He jumped at the sound, his heart kicking up a notch. The sign clearly said they were closed, but the knocking was persistent.

Ethan walked to the front of the store, grabbing a box of cookies while he went. They weren't opening that day, but if someone was brave enough to try the store, Ethan was going to reward them.

He was almost to the door when he recognized the hooded figure standing outside. The hunch of her shoulders was clear. Ethan slid the box of cookies onto one of the round tables. Lizzy was definitely not going to be interested in them.

Opening the door took no effort, but plastering a smile on his face was difficult to do. He knew he and Lizzy had had their differences, but he didn't think she was the kind of person who gloated.

"What can I do for you?" He forced his words to be polite, even though he wondered how much worse the day could get.

The expression on Lizzy's face was one Ethan hadn't seen before. She paused on the doorstep. "Can I come in for a minute?"

Ethan stood to the side, pushing himself against the frame of the door while she passed. He hoped that whatever he had done this time, she would be able to forgive him quickly. The day was already ruined without a lecture from Lizzy.

She pushed the hood off her head and Ethan had to catch his breath. Her cheeks were red with the cold, even down to the tip of her nose. He didn't have any right to be feeling the flutters that flowed through his body, but she still captured his attention.

Lizzy shifted back and forth, crossing and uncrossing her arms. Ethan waited for her to speak, but she was silent.

He decided to break the ice. "Look, it's been a long day already. I'm not sure what I did wrong this time, but I just don't have it in me to argue with you right now. What do you need?"

The question hit the mark. Lizzy opened her mouth to retort, but quickly closed it again. Then she did the last thing Ethan expected. She stepped forward until she was inches away from his body before she stopped. She was close enough for Ethan to be able to study the snowflakes that were dripping down the front of her hair where the hood hadn't covered.

Lizzy placed a hand on his arm. "I'm sorry about today. I was checking to see if I could help with anything."

There had to be a trap somewhere in her words. If he had learned anything from the past, he knew he should turn Lizzy's help down, but he was too tired to banter.

"I don't think that's wise. As you can see, I'm pretty much in the dark here. I don't know when the power will be back on."

"I know. I saw that the entire street is out. Well, your side of the street."

Ethan held back a frustrated sigh. "I'm guessing you saw the sign. We had to cancel the grand opening. You win."

Lizzy gave his arm a small pat before letting go. "I think on a day like today, there are no winners or losers. We're all just business owners trying to help each other out. So, what can I do?"

A surge of warmth filled Ethan's body. He had been trying to be friends with Lizzy for weeks, but she hadn't budged. It was hard to know if she was sincere, but he chose to trust her.

"What are you doing with all your cookies from today?" Ethan gestured to the counter behind him. "If you guys are like us, I'm sure you have dozens of cookies and no customers."

Lizzy nodded. "I was thinking about dropping them off

at the hospital. I know the workers there are probably overwhelmed."

That was an idea that Ethan hadn't considered. "I like it. I was thinking about the homeless shelter, but on a day like today, I'm not sure that's what they need."

There was a brief pause before Lizzy shrugged out of her coat, laying it across the back of a chair. "Where are Kitty and Chad?"

Ethan was surprised she knew the names of his employees. "They went home. I wanted them to get there safely before the storm got too much worse."

"I sent Maria and Robert home, too. I'm still not sure if that was the best decision, but what else was I supposed to do? I can't hold them hostage all day while we wait for two or three customers to come in."

"I know. I keep waiting for them to text that they made it home okay."

Lizzy held out her phone. "Me, too."

A loud thump echoed through the wall. It took Ethan a second to place where the sound had come from, but when he did, his stomach fell. "That's Irma Mae's shop."

A small cloud crossed Lizzy's face. "Do you think she really came in today?" She was reaching for her coat at the same time as Ethan. He held it out for her to slide her hands into the sleeves, ignoring the flutter in his chest when he helped move her hair to the side.

"I hope not, but we'd better check anyway. One sec." Ethan ran to the back office to grab his own coat and the keys. The entire transaction took less than a minute, but

Ethan's nerves were on fire. He needed to make sure Irma Mae was okay.

The world looked like a snow globe when Ethan opened the door for Lizzy. They stepped into the storm, not caring that they were being pelted with snowflakes. It wasn't a far distance to Irma's quilt shop, but every step seemed to take forever.

The shop was dark from the power outage, but Ethan peered inside the window anyway. A small figure was crumpled on the ground near the wall. Ethan tried the door, but it was locked. He rapped on the window, but the figure didn't look up.

"Should we call the paramedics?" Lizzy's voice was soft against the raging storm.

"Yes, but I'm not sure they can get here. I'll go try her back door."

Lizzy's hand was on his arm again. There were layers of jackets and gloves between them, but he still felt a flicker of excitement at her touch.

"Be safe," she said.

Ethan ducked his head and walked back to his store. It was a shortcut to walk through his own shop and approach the quilt shop from the back. A sense of urgency pressed him forward. He needed to make sure the sweet old lady was okay.

The doorknob was sticking when Ethan tried to open it, but he jiggled the handle and bumped it with his shoulder until it swung open. That was something Irma

Mae would want to get looked at later, but for now, he was grateful that he could break in.

He ran to the front of the store, calling Irma's name. "Are you okay?"

The only answer was a small moan. Ethan sprinted to the front door, unlocking the door for Lizzy so she could help. Then he ran to the small heap on the ground.

Irma Mae was laying on the floor, her leg splayed out at an unnatural angle. Lizzy reached for her head. "Irma Mae, it's Lizzy and Ethan. Can you talk?"

The elderly lady lifted her head. "I fell."

"We heard the thump." Ethan held his arm out to help her sit up, but she didn't take it. "Are you okay?" Did you hurt something?"

Irma Mae shook her head. "I don't think I should move. Can you call someone for help?"

"We already did." Lizzy held Irma Mae's hand.

Ethan took a moment to study the room, trying to piece together what happened. A small step stool was flipped upside down near Irma's foot. Bolts of red Christmas fabric tilted at an odd angle. This appeared to be where she tried to break her fall.

Looking at the wall, Ethan knew what had happened. "Irma Mae, were you trying to hang one of your quilts?"

She nodded. "We ran out of quilt kits for the quilt that was on display. I was trying to hang the new one up."

"What about your grandsons?" Ethan asked.

"I told them not to come in today."

Lizzy straightened a bolt of fabric. "Why did you come in? The weather is awful."

Irma Mae's cheeks pinked up. "When the bus came to get me, I didn't even think about it. We get snow here. I figured it would melt away like it usually does."

In the distance, the blaring of sirens was growing louder. "That sounds like your ride," Lizzy said. "I'll go wave at them, so they get the right shop."

Ethan nodded, the weight on his shoulders lifting now that Irma Mae was going to get help. He was impressed with Lizzy and her ability to think quickly under pressure. She was showing him an incredibly caring side. Maybe there was more to Lizzy than he had given her credit for.

After what felt like an eternity, the paramedics came in to assess the situation, quickly taking control. "It looks like you might have fractured your hip," one of the women said. "We're going to need a stretcher."

Two men ran into the snow, bringing in a backboard. Ethan and Lizzy pulled the fabric bolts out of the aisle so there was room for the paramedics to work.

Ethan's fingers twitched to help more. He watched as the paramedics placed the board by Irma Mae's side, gently rolling her so they could slip the board under. Once she was strapped in, they lifted her into the air.

"But what about my shop?" Irma Mae had been relatively quiet, but now she was getting agitated.

"We'll take care of things." Ethan said. He clasped her hand. "Where are the keys so I can lock up?"

Irma Mae waved towards the counter. "They are on a hook behind the cutting table."

Lizzy pressed a hand to her leg. "Don't worry about anything. We'll check on you later."

Irma's tense hand relaxed. "Thank you. Both of you."

The paramedics carried Irma Mae out to the ambulance. Ethan waited until she was loaded, and they were driving away before he spoke.

"Do you think they will get her to the hospital okay?"

Lizzy patted the ear of a fabric bear that sat in a rocking chair at the front of the store. "I sure hope so."

CHAPTER 7

❄

There was a companionable silence in the quilt shop when the door closed. Lizzy turned the knob to lock the door. She looked at Ethan, who gave a small smile. "I can't believe she came in to work today."

"I think she's lonely at home. She's told me before that the shop is her happy place."

Lizzy's heart felt a pang of remorse. How often had she neglected to look in on her own grandma over the years? Was her grandma going to start taking buses in awful weather because she was lonely?

Ethan headed to the fabric wall, where he began to wrap the fabric around each bolt before carefully putting it back in place. The care he took with each bolt showed the concern he felt for the elderly woman. That was part of the community that Lizzy wanted to create between the shop owners.

She felt another pang, this time of guilt. Ethan had tried

to reach out, but all Lizzy had done was reject his efforts. She had been so worried about getting her shop off the ground, she had forgotten her manners somewhere along the way. Thinking about some of the things she said made her cringe with embarrassment.

Lizzy joined Ethan's side; her mouth suddenly dry. She had gone to his shop to extend a peace offering, but she hadn't planned on being part of a rescue project. In the time it had taken to get Irma off to the hospital, Lizzy's walls had crumbled completely down.

She reached for a bolt of fabric, handing it to Ethan. He looked down at her, his eyes vast pools of blue, and heat raced to her heart. It had been a long time since she had allowed herself to feel even the slightest bit of a crush on a man. Now feelings were stirring that would slam them right past friendship into more serious territory.

It didn't take long to straighten up Irma Mae's shop. The final step was Ethan climbing on the stool to hang the quilt that was hanging askew. Lizzy's heart skipped a beat when Ethan turned his head to ask her opinion.

"Does it look right?" he asked.

Lizzy swallowed. There was a double meaning to the question that she was pretty sure he didn't intend. Her view from the ground looked quite good, including the man who towered above her on the stepstool.

She turned her focus to the quilt. "It, uh, is almost there." She took a few steps back. "Pull it a couple of inches to the right and you'll be good."

Ethan slid the quilt over, gently handling the fabric, and

Lizzy's heart melted. He clearly cared about how Irma would feel when she came back to the shop.

There was another awkward silence when Ethan climbed down off the stool. "I'm half tempted to take this back to my shop," he chuckled. "Maybe it will keep Irma out of trouble."

Lizzy tried to frown but it was too difficult to do when she was laughing. "I'm not sure you want to add larceny to your list. If anyone came by, they'd think we were trespassing."

Ethan stashed the stool behind the counter and then leaned down. When he stood back up, he was holding a lanyard in his hand. "At least we can say we have the keys."

Lizzy followed him out the back door over to his shop, feeling self-conscious as she stood on the stoop. Entering Ethan's store through the front was something anyone in the community would do. Entering from the back felt more personal, like she was being invited into his private world.

The snow hadn't let up when Ethan turned to look at her. "Are you coming in?"

Lizzy clutched her coat and ducked her head, fighting against the wind that had picked up.

The temperature inside Ethan's shop had dropped while they were next door. Whatever had caused the power outage didn't seem to be getting fixed any time soon. She shrugged out of her coat, only to pull it back on. It was too cold.

Stacks of cookies sat on trays, waiting for the surge of

customers that Ethan had been expecting. There was a prickle of anxiety that gnawed at her stomach. If the dates had been swapped, she would have been the store owner sitting in a shop with no customers.

She felt awful for him. She had been so focused on being the best, she had never asked him why he opened his shop in the first place. There was no way it had been to compete with her. He wouldn't have known what shop she was planning to open when he was trying to choose his store front.

Lizzy pulled off her gloves, trying to hide a shiver as the cold air hit her hands. She headed to the sink, giving her hands a good scrub before she reached for a spatula that was hanging on the wall.

"Do you want to save any of these for your opening day?" Lizzy had to begrudgingly admit that Ethan's cookie selection looked fantastic.

"You know I can't. They wouldn't be fresh baked." Ethan's forehead creased with frown lines. "I guess I could save some of them to sell for half price, but I don't want that to be people's first impression of my shop."

His words were light, but Lizzy could hear the undercurrent of sadness. The cookies represented hours of work, as well as a lifetime of hopes and dreams. "Let's box them up and you can decide what to do with them while we work."

Ethan reached for a box and began to crease the edges. When he looked up, his eyes were sad. "You don't have to help. I know you have your own shop to take care of. It's a bad day for both of us."

Lizzy nodded. "I was thinking about that. It goes much faster if two people are working on the same job. How would you feel about coming over to help me after we get things taken care of here?"

She held her breath, wanting him to say yes. It wasn't so much that she needed the help, but she was interested in spending more time with Ethan. After months of keeping her distance, it was time to get to know the man instead of judging him.

Ethan ran a hand through his hair. "I don't know. If I come to your shop I might be tempted to steal all your cookies. I'm not sure if I have enough of them here."

His eyes crinkled when she shook the spatula at his face. "If you're a good helper, maybe I'll let you try one of them."

Instead of laughing like Lizzy expected, Ethan's smile faded away. "I'd really like that. Would it make you uncomfortable?"

Lizzy took her time to answer instead of blurting out false platitudes. "Not at all. I haven't behaved like I wanted to in the past. I'm hoping we can have a different relationship moving forward."

She turned her attention to the box he handed her, stacking the cookies in a single layer. She reached for the parchment paper squares on the counter and covered the first layer of cookies, adding a second layer to the top. It wasn't how they'd sell them, but it would waste less of Ethan's boxes.

The box was filled completely before Lizzy registered that Ethan hadn't given her an answer about their relationship moving forward. She slid the box across the counter before looking up.

"Can you tell me why you disliked me so much?" Ethan's eyes held a shadow of hurt.

The question didn't have an easy answer. "I'm not sure I have an answer that would make sense to you. I guess it all boils down to a fear of failure."

"I get that." Ethan handed her another box. "I'm afraid of failing, too."

Lizzy slid a new tray of cookies onto the counter. "It goes deeper than that." She placed a cookie in the corner of the box. "My aunt and uncle lived with us when I was young."

Talking about her history was easier while her hands were busy. She passed another full box of cookies to Ethan, taking an empty one in exchange.

"I thought I was the luckiest girl ever because they were always around. It took several years for me to realize that they weren't living with us because they thought it would be fun. Instead, my uncle kept opening one business after another, sinking all their life's savings into the newest company. They were staying with us because he finally lost their family house."

"That sounds difficult," Ethan said. "What happened to him?"

Lizzy finished clearing the tray and walked it to the sink. The dishes were going to have to wait until Ethan had power again, so her hands didn't freeze.

"They eventually got a business going, but it took a couple of years before they could move out. I was so scared to start selling cookies out of my apartment when I graduated. I thought I'd end up like them. It took a lot of faith to venture out on my own."

Ethan gestured to the boxes they were filling. "So today really isn't going how you expected it to go."

"Nope." Lizzy glanced out the window. "What about you?"

"What do you want to know?" Ethan had assembled a small stack of boxes. He walked to the oven next to Lizzy and pulled out a new tray of cookies.

"Why did you decide to open a cookie shop?"

Ethan stretched his hands above his head and then put them on his waist, twisting from side to side. "It has always been a dream of mine to open a shop. My mom says I was helping her bake in the kitchen from the time I was old enough to hold a spoon. I grew up watching her cook. When I was little, I'd level each scoop of sand in the sandbox before dumping it out."

Lizzy could imagine a small, brown-haired boy running around the sandbox. He was probably incredibly adorable with his big blue eyes.

"When did you decide to open your shop?"

Ethan studied Lizzy's face, as if he was weighing what to say. "This isn't my first shop."

That was news to Lizzy. "What happened to your other shop?"

There was another stretch of silence. "I had to get away from the city."

Questions were swirling through Lizzy's mind, but she didn't want to press Ethan to say more. His tone made it clear that there was more to the story than simply wanting a change of scenery, but she wasn't going to pry.

"Does it sound strange to say that I'm glad you're here?"

Ethan turned the full force of his gaze on her. "Me too. I first thought you were coming to yell at me for intentionally making it snow."

That was a mild blow that Lizzy completely deserved. "I'm sorry for the way I've acted. I was so afraid of my store failing, I didn't take the time to think that you might have a story, too."

Ethan closed the box on the cookies and slid it to the side. "I'm sorry, too."

The apology was unexpected. "You have nothing to apologize for."

"I'll admit that I kind of enjoyed goading you on a little bit. I knew you were struggling, and I turned it into a game instead of getting to know you better."

He stopped working and turned to face Lizzy. "I'm genuinely sorry for my part in this, too."

Words were swirling through Lizzy's mind, but she was lacking the focus to pull them out of the air when his eyes were looking into hers so intently. "Can we call this a truce, then?" Her voice was soft. She meant the words, even if she didn't imagine she'd be saying them earlier in the day.

"I would like that a lot." Ethan held his hand out.

Trails of heat flooded her body when she pressed her hand to his. "I'd like that a lot, too."

The air inside the shop dropped another few degrees. Lizzy tried to hide her shiver, but Ethan's eyes were too sharp. "How about we take this party to your shop. You have heat over there, right?"

Lizzy nodded. She could see the snow swirling outside the windows, a perfect match to the butterflies swirling inside her stomach. The thought of Ethan visiting, as a friend instead of the competition, seemed right, somehow.

She put the last of the cookies from her tray in a box and closed it. "We can finish up here when the power goes on."

The snowplow had passed through a half hour ago, but already the street was covered in another two inches of snow. Cars slowly snaked by, following one thready patch of tire treads that wove down the center of each lane.

Ethan paused outside the door of his shop, locking the door before pocketing his own set of keys as well as Irma Mae's. He bent his elbow. "Are you ready for a mad dash across the street?"

Lizzy rested her hand in the crook of his arm. The first step she took, her feet slipped out on the snow. She shrieked while she began to fall, but Ethan's arm was there to steady her. He glanced at her face and then turned away, hiding a smirk.

"Would you settle for a slow shuffle?" Lizzy didn't think her shoes were made for dashing anywhere.

"That sounds better." Ethan waited while she readjusted her grasp before they set off.

Lizzy tried to focus on putting one foot in front of the other rather than questioning what the day was coming to mean. In a matter of minutes, she'd be in her shop, with Ethan behind the counter helping her.

Walking across the street was a balancing act that took all Lizzy's coordination. She'd step in one spot and the snow would pack down nicely under her feet. The next step her foot would catch a hidden patch of ice and it would go flying out from under her. She was laughing uncontrollably when they got to the other side of the street.

"I can't believe we made it," Lizzy said. She let go of Ethan's arm, but his face furrowed.

"Are you sure you want to do that? We still have to make it down the sidewalk."

"Good point." Lizzy curled her hand around his arm once more, her thoughts wandering. She was curious what it would feel like to walk arm and arm with Ethan in a real relationship. He would be the sort of guy who would take care of her, even in a storm.

Lizzy let go when they reached the front of her shop. She hadn't bothered locking the door because she had gone over to Ethan's shop without a real plan. It was a neighborly thing to do to check on him, but the day was unfolding far differently than she could have imagined.

"Welcome to Cookies by Liz." Lizzy swung open the door, studying Ethan's face as he crossed the threshold. He scanned the shop appraisingly, his gaze lingering on the cookie tray displaying the current flavors of the week.

"I know we're competitors and all, but those sugar cookies look incredible." Ethan was pointing to the cookie which was shaped like a turkey.

"I was hoping to sell the rest of them for Thanksgiving this week. Next week we'll have a new design to celebrate Christmas."

"Where did you learn to decorate cookies like that?" The admiration in Ethan's voice was easy to hear.

"You said you started baking with your mom when you were young. I had the opposite. My mom was an awful cook. You know how people joke about being able to burn a pot of boiling water?"

Ethan nodded.

"That was an almost daily occurrence for her. It didn't matter if it was spaghetti, pancakes, or something in between. She always managed to mess it up. I was doing all the cooking for the family by the time I was ten. In junior high, I took a baking class. That's when I discovered how much I love baking."

"And you've been doing it ever since." Ethan ran a hand through his hair. "I can bake, but I can't decorate. A swirl of frosting on top of a round cookie is about all I can manage."

Lizzy had just spent the past hour in and out of Ethan's shop. "You may not be a decorator, but the flavors in your shop smelled divine. I've been thinking about the molasses cookie you gave me ever since that day."

"That was my grandma's recipe. I've been trying to recreate the flavors for weeks. I think I finally got it right. I was so excited for the customers to taste them." His face fell, and Lizzy was reminded that this wasn't just a regular day, hanging out with a new friend. Today was a loss for both of them, but Ethan had it the worst.

"I can't believe your opening day was snowed out." Lizzy shook her head. "You seem to be handling it a lot better than I think I would be."

Ethan sighed. "I don't know how else to react. I mean, I could blame the weather, but what is the good in that? It isn't like the storm came through on purpose to ruin my day."

"Oh, I can think of a few natural responses. Disappointment. Anger. Sadness. That's how I was feeling before I came to your shop."

Ethan shrugged out of his coat and cocked his head towards a white chair. "Is it okay to set this down here?"

Lizzy nodded. "Of course."

"So how are you feeling now?"

Lizzy trailed her fingers along the countertop. "Honestly? My time with you has given me a much-needed perspective shift. I mean, thinking about Irma Mae makes my heart hurt. We're losing business today, but she's potentially facing surgery. If she really broke something, she'll be out of work for weeks. We'll be out of work for a day or two."

"You're right." Ethan headed to Lizzy's side. "So how about we get this party started?"

Lizzy laughed and tossed a lavender apron over to Ethan. She tried to tell herself that the flutters going through her body were purely gratitude, but even she didn't believe the lie.

In one day, the enemy she was determined to beat was now becoming her friend. They could get back to the competition tomorrow, but today, they were going to be a team. Thinking of them together felt way better than it should.

Ethan reached for a box, and Lizzy's heart spattered out an uneven beat. He looked good standing in her cookie kitchen. A little too good. She turned her focus to the trays of cookies waiting behind her. The faster she got this job done, the sooner she'd be able to stop thinking about Ethan.

That couldn't come soon enough.

CHAPTER 8

❄

*I*f someone had told Ethan that his opening day would turn out as a chaotic disaster, and that he'd spend the day washing dishes in Lizzy's shop, he would have called them a liar. There was no way he'd spend that much time with the woman who had deliberately avoided him. Now, he couldn't imagine having a better outcome to a terrible day.

He was washing a cookie tray when he heard a loud crash, followed by the shattering of glass. Ethan's stomach sank when he met eyes with Lizzy. They ran to the front of the store together and peered out.

Down the street, a car was tilted at an unnatural angle, jutting into the road. The front bumper was smashed into the side of a parked car. Steam rose from the hood.

"Are you ready to put on your superhero cape again?" Ethan asked, but Lizzy was already reaching for her coat.

She ran behind the counter and pulled out a small red bag. "It isn't much, but we might need a first aid kit."

Ethan reached for her hand, clasping it tightly while they made their way through high drifts of snow. Each pass of the snowplow had thrown more snow onto the sidewalks, but no one was out with shovels to clear the path. Every second it took to get to the car felt like an eternity as Ethan watched the door, waiting for it to open and the driver to step out.

"He should be climbing out," Lizzy said. "What if the car explodes?"

"I know." Ethan squeezed her hand. "We're almost there."

"Should we call 9-1-1?"

Ethan shook his head. "I'm sure the paramedics have been slammed with calls. I don't want them to head here unless it is a true emergency. Let's see how the driver is doing first."

The snow whipped against their faces. Ethan held one hand out to block the wind, but it wasn't helping. He lowered his hand when he got to the car.

The front side of the car looked far worse up close. Lizzy gasped beside him. "I'm afraid to see what's inside."

"Me too." He wanted to protect Lizzy. "I can check first, if you want."

It was completely understandable that Lizzy was freaked out. He was too. He took a breath and reached for the door, pulling it towards him. The airbags on the car hadn't triggered, which meant the driver hadn't been going too fast.

A slender woman looked up at him, her eyes wide with shock. "The car. It just started sliding. I don't know what happened."

"Are you okay?" Lizzy was standing at Ethan's side. He hadn't realized she followed. She clutched her first aid kit in one hand and leaned against the door.

"I crashed my husband's car." The woman wrung her hands together, her body shaking.

"What is your name?" Ethan asked.

"Elsie."

"Elsie, I'm Ethan and this is my friend Lizzy. Are you hurt anywhere?"

Elsie held her arms out in front of her, turning them from side to side. "I don't see any blood."

"That's good. How about your back and your neck? Is there any pain when you move them?"

Elsie shook her head from side to side. She leaned forward and back in the seat before turning to Ethan. "I don't feel anything."

He glanced over his shoulder at Lizzy. "Can we take her to your shop so she can get out of the cold?"

Lizzy rested her hand on his arm. "Of course. Anything to help."

The wind was blowing past them, swirling snow into the car. It was difficult to see the street. He reached out a hand. "Elsie, I think it would be best if we can get you out of the car. My friend Lizzy owns a cookie shop that is right down this sidewalk. Would you like to go there to wait?"

Elsie shook her head. "I hit a car. I'm not going to be part of a hit and run. What if the owner comes back?"

"We can keep an eye out from my shop." Lizzy gestured to Ethan's outstretched hand. "Why don't you unbuckle your seatbelt and come with us? We can call the police from my shop, and they can come here when they have the time."

Giant tears welled up in Elsie's eyes. "But what about the car? What will I tell my husband?"

Ethan smiled when Lizzy patted her shoulder. "I think he'll be relieved that you are okay." She moved out of Ethan's way, letting him step to the car.

He grabbed Elsie's arm to steady her while she climbed out. She shivered, and Ethan realized that the woman was wearing a thin dress. He glanced around the car, heaving a breath of relief when he saw a fur-lined coat sitting on the seat beside her.

He passed her to Lizzy and then climbed across the seat, grabbing the coat. Elsie's hands shook as he helped her into the jacket. "Do you need anything else from the car?"

"My purse, please."

Ethan took it out of the car and walked to the other side of Elsie's body. Together, he and Lizzy escorted her to the cookie shop. They got her settled at a table and Lizzy walked behind the counter, bringing a couple of cookies to their guest.

She lifted her eyebrows at Ethan, jerking her head towards the other chair. Ethan got the unspoken message. Someone needed to stay by Elsie. He sank to the seat, pulling out his phone. "Would you like to call the police now?"

Elsie shook her head. "I don't know what to say."

"It's okay. I can help." Elsie reminded Ethan of his mom, who always got rattled in uncomfortable situations.

Ethan was on hold when Lizzy walked back over. She placed a couple of cookies in front of him with a wry smile.

Spending time with Lizzy was stirring up complicated feelings. He was getting more and more smitten with the woman in front of him. The tension from the past couple of months had faded while they worked together to help each other.

Elsie stared at him intently while he made the call, her cookies untouched in front of her. Ethan lifted a cookie to his mouth, and she copied him. She was clearly still in shock.

It took a minute for the flavors to hit his tongue. When they did, Ethan leaned back with a small moan. He called out to Lizzy. "You know these are delicious, right?"

She looked up from behind the counter where she was boxing cookies. A hint of a smile danced across her lips. "Thanks."

Ethan glanced at Elsie. She had stopped shaking and was scrolling her phone, lost in her own thoughts while she nibbled on her cookie. "Are you okay here?" he asked. "I want to see if Lizzy needs any help."

Elsie nodded her head.

The police had said they would be there as soon as they could, but it might take up to an hour. Ethan didn't plan to spend an hour sitting at a table with someone who was fine. He wanted to keep his promise to Lizzy to help.

He walked to her side and leaned down to whisper in her ear. "Our friend is content for now. What can I do back here?"

Lizzy handed him a stack of boxes, but then she paused. "I was planning to send a bunch of cookies back with the officers when they come. Do you want to grab a few boxes from your shop to send as well?"

Ethan knew that sending free boxes of cookies to an establishment was great advertising. The fact that Lizzy wanted to share that opportunity with him filled him with a surge of appreciation.

"Do you feel comfortable alone here with Elsie?" He kept his voice low so their visitor wouldn't hear, but he wanted to make sure Lizzy felt safe.

She smiled and reached for his hand. "I'll be fine. Don't take too long, though. I don't want to have to drag you back here if you turn into a popsicle."

Ethan squeezed her hand. "I'll hurry." He pushed out the front door, carrying the warmth from Lizzy with him.

Crossing the street proved to be more difficult than he imagined. He took a few steps forward only to realize that the snow was falling so fast, he couldn't see very far in front of his face. On a sunny day, it was easy to cross the street, timing it to make sure no cars were coming. Now he wasn't sure he even trusted the traffic light on the corner.

Ethan stood near the crosswalk, straining his ears to hear if there was a rumble of cars coming from either direction. He waited until a car crawled past before he strode across the street. One half of his mission was done.

Stepping into his store he was met with a blast of cold air. Cookie bakeries were usually warm and inviting, but his store made him shudder. He missed the light and the warmth of the ovens.

Ethan stacked up several boxes of cookies. It would be easier to take multiple trips, but he wasn't sure he wanted to head out in the storm more than once. He was going to have to be content with everything he could carry in one trip.

He was almost back to Lizzy's shop when he noticed her waiting at the door for him, a smile tugging at her lips. She pulled the door open, stepping to the side so he could squeeze past.

Ethan set the boxes down on the counter and headed to Elsie's side. "How are you feeling now?"

She looked up at him with a smile. "Much better. Your girlfriend was telling me about Irma Mae. Do you think she'll be okay?"

The word girlfriend was a new one to him. He stiffened, trying to think what would give Elsie that impression. Were his new feelings for Lizzy starting to show? He glanced Lizzy's way to see that she was biting the side of her cheek. It looked like she was trying not to laugh.

"I think Irma's in good hands. Did my, uh, girlfriend tell you anything else?"

Elsie began to squirm in her seat as she looked at Lizzy. "That's between us ladies."

Ethan could guess what happened. The ladies had concocted a prank while he was gone. Well, two could play that game. Ethan walked to Lizzy's side, wrapping his arm around her waist. She froze for just a second before leaning into his touch.

Standing with his arm around her felt comfortable, like she was made to snuggle into his side. He resisted the urge to press a cheek to her hair.

"It sounds like you gals had a great chat while I was gone. What else did you tell her, *sweetheart?*" He emphasized the word.

Lizzy pressed her lips together, trying to keep a straight face. She couldn't do it. A short laugh burst out, echoed by laughter coming from Elise.

"Sorry, Ethan. Elsie asked if we were dating, and the prank kind of snowballed from there. It was worth it to see the expression on your face."

Ethan smacked a hand across his forehead. "You got me."

It felt good to have Lizzy teasing him. That was something real friends would do. Ethan was opening his mouth to tease her back when another sickening thud met his ears. He locked eyes with Lizzy.

"Not again." She was reaching for her coat when Elsie began to cry.

"What is happening?" Her tears were falling fast, and Ethan realized that the shock hadn't worn off completely.

He walked to her side, pressing down on her shoulder. "We're going to go see if someone else needs help like you did. Can you keep an eye on the shop?"

It wasn't going to do anyone any good if Elsie trailed along in her condition. Giving her a job would hopefully help keep her calm.

She sniffed and rubbed her nose. "I guess so." She looked at Lizzy. "What do I do if someone wants to buy something?"

Lizzy patted her hand. "We won't be gone that long. If someone comes in, you can help them pick the flavors of cookie they'd like."

Ethan liked how quickly Lizzy thought on her feet. He opened the door and held his arm out for her to grab.

"We really should stop going out in the storm like this," he said when her feet began to slip.

Lizzy nodded, clasping his arm with both hands. "I'm just glad you have good shoes. I'm going to have to start keeping winter boots in the office for snowy days."

When they got closer to the wreck, it was easy to see what had caused the bang. Elsie's car had been jutting out in the road, and with the limited visibility from the storm, another car plowed right into it. Ethan was glad the police were on their way because this was a mess that was going to need to be cleared up soon.

The first car door was opening before Ethan and Lizzy got there. An overweight man clambered out, pulling on a jacket. "That car appeared out of thin air. We've got to check the driver."

"It's okay, sir. We already got her out." Ethan glanced at the road in time to see pale headlights heading towards them. "Everyone get to the sidewalk, now."

They moved out of the way right before a truck crashed into the first gentleman's car, followed by another heavy thud from behind the truck that made the truck shudder. And that thud started a chain reaction.

When the crashes stopped, Ethan counted seven cars in a crumpled line, with varying degrees of damage. A quick assessment showed small dents in the fenders of the larger cars to more serious damage to the bodies of the smaller cars. It was difficult to see just how extensive the damage was with the snow billowing around them.

Ethan and Lizzy went from car to car, checking on the drivers. By the time they got everyone out and headed back to the shop, there were a dozen people sitting at tables.

Lizzy reached for a box of Ethan's cookies, pulling the lid open.

"What are you doing?" he asked. "All these people are in your shop. You should feed them your cookies." He didn't want to take away potential customers from her. Especially not when she had been so gracious opening her doors.

She reached for his hand, giving it a gentle squeeze that blasted him with heat before she let go. "Today was supposed to be your opening day. It would be a shame to not have anyone taste your cookies."

The offer was extremely generous. If the situation was

reversed, would Ethan be willing to do the same? He hoped so.

Ethan could read the sincerity in her eyes. "We can give them both of our cookies."

He cleared his throat and turned to face the small crowd, standing close to Lizzy's side. "I know today has been jarring for all of you. As we told you when you headed to the store, the police are already on their way. They should be here soon. In the meantime, we'd like to invite you to be part of our first official taste test."

He looked down at Lizzy's face, glad he was getting to see the generous person she was. "My generous friend Lizzy, here, is the amazing owner of this shop. I think you are going to love her cookies."

Lizzy stepped forward. "What you don't know is that my talented friend Ethan is the owner of the cookie shop across the street. If the power was out on this side instead of his, I know you'd be sitting over there instead. So today you get to try both of our cookies."

Three young girls with sandy blonde hair cheered. Their mother looked at Ethan and Lizzy with relief. "Thank you," she said. "I can't believe we got into a wreck."

Ethan set several cookies in the middle of the table. "This snowstorm is unlike anything I've ever seen. From the reports we've heard, you guys are just one of many different accidents around the city. I'm glad you're safe."

"Me too. Thanks again."

Ethan circled to another table to check on the next set of people. As he talked to them, he kept tabs on Lizzy out of the corner of his eye. She was taking time to talk to each person, leaving them with a pat on the shoulder or a hug. Ethan wasn't sure if there was a way to fast track a relationship, but he knew that before he left today, he planned to ask Lizzy out on a date.

A half hour later, the flash of red and blue lights outside found Ethan reaching for his coat once more. The door swung open, and two officers walked in, saving Ethan the trip outside.

The first officer stood eye to eye with Ethan. He held out his hand. "I'm Officer Grandy, and this is Officer Taft. We're sorry for the wait."

Officer Grandy looked around the store. "Who owns this shop?"

Lizzy stepped forward. "That would be me. I'm Lizzy Thompson."

He shook her hand. "Thank you for your quick response to the accidents, and for taking these people in. On days like today, it helps us a lot when the community watches out for each other."

Ethan stepped back to give her room, but Lizzy pulled him forward. "This is Ethan Crandall. I couldn't have done any of this without his help."

Officer Taft gripped his hand tightly. "Thanks to both of you. It is going to take us a while to process everyone. Do you mind if we use your shop as a base of operations?"

Lizzy pointed to the last remaining table. "It's all yours. Would you like some cookies while you work?"

She said the magic words. Lizzy winked at Ethan while

the officers walked to their table. "Ready for two more customers?"

Ethan nodded. He carried the cookies over to the officers, making sure to present Lizzy's cookies first. "She's pretty amazing," he told the officers.

"We'll try to get everyone out of your hair as soon as possible." Officer Grandy took a bite of the sugar cookie, his eyes opening wide. "This is delicious."

Officer Taft was holding one of Ethan's molasses cookies. "So is mine."

Ethan met Lizzy in the kitchen where she was washing a tray. "Well, the good news is that the officers love our cookies. If you ever get a speeding ticket, maybe you could pay it off in cookies."

Lizzy gave an exaggerated gasp, clutching her hand to her heart. "Are you suggesting that I bribe an officer of the law?"

"Maybe." Ethan reached for a sponge. He was starting to feel the weight of the day crashing down, but there was no way he was going to head home before Lizzy's store was cleaned up. "I'm just saying, we may have an out if things go sideways."

Lizzy started laughing. "Would you believe that I've never gotten a speeding ticket before in my life?"

Her brown eyes flickered to his, and he put his hands in the suds, unsure what to think. "After everything that's happened today, I'm going to choose to believe you. I'm guessing you don't like to cause trouble."

"Nope." Lizzy reached for the pan that Ethan had

washed, rinsing it under the running faucet. Even washing dishes, they worked well together as a team. "My older brother used to drive me to school when we were kids. He drove like a maniac all the time. I stopped counting all the times he scared me half to death."

"That would do it." Ethan handed a spatula to Lizzy to rinse. "I guess you don't have to worry about speeding anywhere today."

Lizzy shook her head. "Nope. I'm not going anywhere until the weather decides to calm down."

Ethan wished he had that option. His store was far too cold to hang out in all day. Lizzy seemed to read his thoughts.

"You're welcome to stay here as long as you'd like."

Forty-five minutes later, when the police had processed all the reports and all the customers had left, Ethan sank to a chair. "Do you feel like this day has lasted forever?"

The snow was finally beginning to ebb, as if the world had finally run out of the moisture to create more flakes.

Lizzy nodded. "It's been at least a million years so far. Maybe more."

"As crazy as it sounds, I'm going to try to head home." Ethan stood, hesitating before he reached for his coat.

"Are you sure?" There was a hint of sadness in her voice. Ethan wondered if she was as reluctant to end their bizarre day together as he was.

"I'm sure. I'm ready to collapse on my feet."

That earned a smile from Lizzy. "I feel the same."

It was so easy to talk to Lizzy now. Over the course of

the day they had gone from being tentative friends to forming a bond that would last for years to come.

Lizzy reached for his hand. "Thanks for everything, today. You were amazing."

"So were you."

Ethan left the warmth of Lizzy's shop, eager to see where the future took him. He still had an opening day to reschedule, and more pressingly, he had to navigate the roads home, but he felt hopeful that things would work out. If nothing else, the woman across the street wasn't going to be a problem anymore.

That was what he told himself when he revved his engine into life. It wasn't until he was driving home that he realized he had an entirely new problem.

He was happy to have made a friend. The problem was that now he had feelings for the woman who was his direct competition. Was there a way to continue to get to know her that wouldn't burn both of them in the process?

CHAPTER 9

❄

*D*riving on the snow-covered roads felt a little like driving through a magical winter wonderland. Lizzy could imagine this was what Santa's elves experienced commuting to the North Pole every day for work. She was glad that this storm had been a fluke and not a normal day.

The slow crawl down the street was giving Lizzy far too much time to think about a certain brown-haired man who happened to feature in all her favorite parts of the day. Watching Ethan work was something that surprised her. He was so good at helping to calm each person, no matter how nervous they seemed to be.

That reminded Lizzy of their first save of the day. Poor Irma Mae was probably still stuck in the hospital. Armed with boxes of cookies, Lizzy turned towards the hospital instead of heading home. Once she knew Irma was okay, then she'd be able to relax.

The hospital parking lot was much less crowded than she expected. It confirmed her suspicions that Irma Mae probably didn't have any visitors.

Lizzy's stomach began to growl when she passed by the cafeteria. All she'd had to eat for the day was cookies, which were delicious but not a substantial meal. She was going to have to remedy that situation after her visit.

As Lizzy got closer to Irma Mae's room, she could hear laughter spilling into the hallway. With a start, Lizzy realized she recognized the voices. She pulled up outside the door, debating if she should go in.

A doctor answered that question when he stepped up beside her. "Are you coming to check on Irma Mae as well?"

Lizzy nodded, taking a small breath as she entered the room behind the doctor.

The hospital room was nondescript, from the same pale wallpaper that seemed to adorn every hospital wall in existence, to the beeping blood pressure monitor that dangled loosely from Irma Mae's arm. The room looked exactly how Lizzy expected, with one exception.

Ethan sat in a chair that he had pulled right up to Irma Mae's bedside. They were talking animatedly about something until the doctor cleared his throat. Ethan's eyes slid from the doctor straight to Lizzy's face, and then he smiled.

He pushed the chair back against the wall and headed for Lizzy's side, giving the doctor room to work.

"It seems like you had the same idea as me," he whispered.

"How is our favorite grandma?" Lizzy's heart was doing somersaults in her chest. There hadn't been any reason to stay at the shop, but she also hadn't been ready to say goodbye to Ethan yet. Now he was here.

Irma Mae glanced Lizzy's way and held out her hand. "Come closer, kids. The doctor was telling me about my hip."

The doctor peered over his spectacles at Lizzy and Ethan. "I'm Doctor Braden. Are you her family?"

Irma Mae scolded him. "They're even better. These two are the ones who saved me. I can only imagine what would have happened if they hadn't been next door to hear my fall."

He held his clipboard out. "Well, you are lucky they were there. I'm afraid I don't have good news."

"I could have told you that." Irma Mae pointed to the I.V. that was dripping into her arm. "They don't give you the good stuff unless it's bad."

That made everyone in the room chuckle. Lizzy squeezed Irma Mae's hand. "Would you like us to give you some privacy so you can talk to the doctor?"

It was a relief when Irma shook her head. "Don't be silly." She turned to the doctor. "How bad is it?"

Dr. Braden pointed to an image on the computer monitor. "You have a fracture, like we suspected. Do you see the dark areas here and here?"

He pointed to the screen and Irma Mae nodded.

"You are going to need surgery to heal properly."

At those words, Irma's eyes began to pool with tears. "But what about my shop? It's almost Christmas time. People need to buy fabric for their projects."

Ethan rested his hand on Irma's shoulder. "What about Dana? She works for you part time, right?"

"Well, yes, but she has a family of her own to take care of. She can't work all the time."

It was heartbreaking watching Irma Mae struggle. Lizzy stroked her hand. "Ethan and I will help keep an eye on your shop until you find someone to step in. I know there are lots of people looking for extra money for the holidays. I'm sure there are at least a couple of quilting fanatics out there who would love to spend time working at the shop."

Irma's face brightened. "I wonder if Wendy would want to help."

Ethan glanced at Lizzy before turning his attention to Irma. "How about you make a list, and we'll get together with Dana to figure it out. Your store will be in good hands."

Doctor Braden cleared his throat and gave them a wry smile. "Now that you have that worked out, can we get back to the scans?"

"Oops. Sorry." Lizzy gave Irma's hand a final squeeze and stepped to the back of the room where Ethan joined her. She leaned in close.

"How are we going to manage Irma's shop along with

ours?" She had made promises but had no clue how to keep them.

Ethan grimaced. "I was thinking the same thing. I have no idea. It's Irma though. How can we walk away?"

His hand hung by his side. Lizzy hesitated for a beat, weighing out her options. Then she reached for his hand, hooking her pinky finger through his. In response, Ethan pressed his body closer to hers. They stood, shoulder to shoulder, until the doctor finished explaining how Irma's next few days would look.

Irma Mae's eyes were drooping while she leaned back on the pillow after the doctor left. Lizzy and Ethan stood on opposite sides of the bed. "You'll be okay," Lizzy said.

"We've got you." Ethan smoothed down Irma's hair and straightened her blanket. "We'll come back tomorrow to see how you're doing."

"Get some rest," Lizzy said. She gave Irma Mae's hand a final squeeze before turning to follow Ethan out of the room.

They didn't speak until they were at the end of the hallway, out of Irma's ear shot for sure.

"The poor lady." Lizzy hated seeing her so vulnerable. "I am so grateful we were there. Otherwise, she could still be laying on the ground."

The thought of it was chilling.

"I can't think about the what ifs. It's too scary." Ethan ran a hand through his hair. "On a different note, I'm starving. I know it's not gourmet food, but do you want to join me in the cafeteria for a bite to eat?"

Lizzy's mouth was watering at the thought. "Oh my gosh. Yes please. I love cookies—"

"—but they're not enough." Ethan finished her sentence with a laugh. "I've been thinking the same thing all day."

The hospital cafeteria had a modest selection of food, but everything looked amazing, from the cheeseburgers to the pizza slices. Lizzy reached for a tray. "Right now, I think I could eat one of everything."

Ethan laughed. "I feel the same. I know people throughout the world are truly starving, but right now, I'm feeling some pretty big hunger pangs."

"Me too." They loaded their trays and walked to the table. Lizzy didn't know how she'd feel sitting so close to Ethan, but she didn't have to worry.

He passed her a napkin when they sat, and then reached for his fork. "So, does this count as an official date? Because after a day like today, I'm pretty sure I'd like to take you out."

Lizzy looked at the chicken enchiladas sitting on her plate, and then over at Ethan's double stack hamburger. "I mean, this is gourmet food, and all, but the setting is a little, well, pedestrian."

"So, you're saying that if I take you out, I need to make sure the restaurant is a fancy one?"

"Obviously. As you can see from my very refined palate, I only eat the best foods life has to offer." She picked up a french fry, laughing while she dipped it in ranch dressing. "I mean, doesn't everyone fancy eat their enchiladas with fries?"

Ethan snagged a fry off her plate. "Honestly, a lot of Mexican food restaurants have fries as a side dish, so this is pretty gourmet. And now we've shared food. Or, rather, I've stolen some of your food. I'm pretty sure that is proper date behavior."

Lizzy leaned her elbows against the table. "I'm not so sure about the ambiance. I mean, I like dressing up before I go out. Most of the customers here seem to have a slightly eccentric style. I mean, seriously, who coordinates to wear blue scrub tops when they go out?"

Ethan crinkled his nose. "True. And the restaurant decor is confusing. What does it say about the food? I'm getting more of a reception room vibe than that of a fine dining establishment."

He took a bite of his burger and then sat back; closing his eyes while he chewed. "Oh my gosh. This burger tastes amazing after the day I've had. Do you want to try a bite?"

He held the burger out and Lizzy's heart raced. Sharing food was something good friends did. Not casual acquaintances. The simple gesture might not mean anything to Ethan, but it meant a lot to Lizzy. It meant he was thinking about her.

She took a bite, trying to savor all the flavors as she chewed. "It's not bad, but my enchiladas are better." Feeling self-conscious, Lizzy slid the tray across the table. Ethan took a bite, chewing slowly.

"I'm afraid we're going to have to agree to disagree. My hamburger clearly has superior flavors." He laughed. "Although your enchiladas are a close second."

"That's okay. I know my cookies take first place." She was teasing, but a shadow crossed Ethan's face.

"I can't believe how many cookies I had to throw away today. We made so many extra to be prepared for the grand opening."

Lizzy's heart ached for her friend. "I know how important today was to you. As much as I wish things had been different, I can't help but feel glad that I got to know you better."

Ethan leaned forward to fold his arms across the table. "No matter what happens with my shop, I'll always be grateful that you came over to check on me. Who knew that we'd end up helping a dozen people?"

"Plus the police officers." Lizzy loved seeing their faces light up. "You can't forget them." They had sent boxes of cookies back to the station.

Lizzy smiled. "I guess the hospital staff is happy as well. I brought the rest of my cookies here."

Ethan's eyes crinkled with laughter. "So did I."

They settled into a companionable silence, although Lizzy kept sneaking glances at Ethan's face. He seemed almost too good to be true.

Physically, Ethan had a perfectly symmetrical face except for a small scar that ran along the edge of one eyebrow. His brown hair was loosely styled, with just a slight wave to give it volume. The eyes that watched her were pools of blue that were easy to sink into.

As an unfair taunt to the rest of the world, Ethan also had Lizzy's favorite body type. He was a medium build,

with a sculpted chest. He had enough muscles to give defi-
nition, but he wasn't so bulky that hugging him would feel
more like hugging a rock.

The physical traits were nice, but Lizzy had been
looking at his perfect face for weeks and never felt the way
she did now. Her heart fluttered whenever Ethan spoke.
Lizzy knew that the real reason she was attracted to Ethan
was because of the way he had acted today.

Somehow, the man knew all the right words to say. He
had been a soft, comforting presence when Irma Mae had
fallen, but he had taken charge when she was worried
about her shop. He had kept a level head when car after car
crashed into each other, helping each driver and passenger
without judgment.

He had every reason to rage at the world. Opening days
were important for any business, but his had bombed spec-
tacularly. Ethan's first shot to reach his dreams had been
foiled, and yet he still managed to look outward and care
for those around him. He was amazing.

"How do you keep such an optimistic attitude?" Lizzy
was trailing another french fry through her dressing. She
looked at Ethan's face. "Today was a disaster by anyone's
standards, and yet I haven't seen you break down yet."

Ethan cupped his hand behind his neck and rubbed it.
"It sounds cheesy, but I think I could handle the disap-
pointments of today for a couple of reasons. The first,
being you. If you hadn't been there to help, I'm not sure
how I would have reacted."

Lizzy shook her head. "Thank you. That's sweet to say,

but there has to be more to it than that. You were keeping it together long before I came over."

A shadow crossed Ethan's face. "I guess I was able to stay calm because I've been through worse. I almost lost my youngest sister when I was seventeen. She was playing with friends and ran into the street at the wrong time. The car didn't have time to stop. By the time the paramedics got to us, we were sure she was gone."

"Oh, I'm so sorry." Lizzy reached for his hand. There was even more to the man than she expected.

"The hardest part was the waiting. We knew Quinn was in bad shape when we took her in, but the doctors all said she'd be fine. They said she'd pull through, but those first few days were agony."

"Is that why you're here, checking on Irma Mae?"

Ethan's body was a statue. "I know she's just the sweet shop owner next door, but I worry about people. I'd feel awful if something had happened to her."

"That isn't silly at all." Lizzy wanted to pinch herself to see if Ethan was actually real.

"I guess, getting back to your question, at the end of the day, cookies are just cookies. I want my shop to succeed more than anything in this world. I think you can relate."

Lizzy nodded.

"But if I let a day like today bring me down, I'd lose focus of the important things in life. I'd forget that behind every customer is a story, and behind most of those stories is a layer of heartache. The day my sister got hit changed the lives of several people. I vowed to never get upset about the things I couldn't control. It hasn't been easy, but it has definitely helped me in my life."

Lizzy pushed back from the table and pretended to walk away. "Forget the date. I'm not worthy to sit by you."

Ethan reached for her arm, pulling her back with a laugh. "Sit down. You know, you were amazing today as well."

"I don't feel like I did anything but call 9-1-1."

"I can help fill in a few pieces. You crossed the street to check on your least favorite shop owner, even though the devastatingly handsome man might be trying to sabotage your business."

She laughed at his description.

"To make matters worse, you had to pair up with the man to make sure a sweet old lady was okay. And then you opened your shop to a dozen customers, keeping their bodies fed and their spirits up. I think you were incredible today, too."

The way Ethan was talking, she sounded like a saint. Lizzy was wrapped in a bubble. She didn't want their last-minute date in the cafeteria to end but the food was disappearing quickly. Sure enough, after a few more minutes passed, Ethan pushed his tray to the side with a sigh.

"I'm ready to get home but I'm not sure I want this day to end. As horrible of a day as it has been, there have been a few really nice parts."

"Like going on an unofficially official first date?" Lizzy loved that part of the day.

Ethan gazed into her eyes. "Exactly."

Flutters kicked Lizzy's pulse up a notch. She was glad she wasn't hooked to any blood pressure monitors, or they'd surely be setting off alarms. She could imagine how the nurses would laugh when she tried to explain why they were going off. *See that handsome guy over there? It's his fault. He had to go all Prince Charming on me and make me swoon.*

It would definitely earn her some good-natured teasing, especially if Ethan was in the room at the time. Thankfully, she wasn't hooked up and he couldn't see how he made her react.

Ethan placed his napkin and water cup on the tray and stood. "Can I take your tray?"

It was another simple gesture that meant a lot. Ethan was thinking about her needs. The thought of how she had treated him in the past crossed her mind once more. She had apologized, but she was determined to show with her actions that she was a changed woman.

Lizzy followed behind Ethan, waiting while he dumped their trash and stacked the trays. The walk out to the parking lot was far too short for Lizzy's liking. All too soon, she was standing next to her car.

Ethan opened the door for her. "Drive safe. I don't want to have to run both cookie shops while they patch you up."

"We'll see. I got several lessons today about how to slide into other cars." Lizzy walked past Ethan to climb in but then she stopped. She turned and rested her hand on his arm. "Thank you for everything today. I won't forget it."

Ethan covered her hand with his, giving it a little

squeeze. "Will you text me when you're home, so I don't have to worry?"

"Only if you do the same."

Lizzy waited in her car until the heater kicked in before beginning the slow drive home. She was pulling on to her street when Ethan's text came through.

Made it safe and sound.

The text was accompanied by a selfie of Ethan giving her a thumbs up.

I just pulled into my driveway. See you soon?

Three dots flashed across the screen. Lizzy was inside her house when his text came through.

I'm planning on it.

CHAPTER 10

❄

*T*wo days later the snow cleared, leaving the streets clear. Ethan met Chad and Kitty at the shop early in the morning. Instead of filling the shop with trays upon trays of cookies, Ethan told them to make the amount they'd use on a regular day. With his grand opening delayed, the odds of getting a full house were low. It was better to not waste money on ingredients for a second time that week.

He was grabbing a bag of powdered sugar from the storage room when Kitty came running back. "Uh, boss? I think you need to see this."

Ethan's stomach sank. He had already delayed his opening by two days. There wasn't room in his body for another setback. Kitty led Ethan to the front of the shop and jerked her head towards the window.

A crowd of faces peered eagerly into the store.

"What is happening?" Ethan asked.

"I think they're here for the shop opening." Kitty waved at the customers and headed back to her station.

"But where did they all come from?" There wasn't a logical explanation for why there were dozens of people suddenly lining up on the street. Ethan felt a rush of excitement followed by a burst of panic.

"Remember how I told you to treat today like a normal one?" Ethan grabbed an apron off the wall and tied it around his waist. "I take that back. Let's fill this store with cookies."

By the time the store opened, the crowd had grown so long that there were people lining up down the sidewalk onto the next block. Ethan didn't have time to question where they were coming from. He put a smile on his face that he hoped to keep until the rush of the crowd died down.

Three hours in, Ethan's shoulders ached from lifting trays of dough and tubs of frosting. He had expected to have a good opening day before the snowstorm ruined everything, but this day was exceeding his wildest dreams.

He didn't get an answer why until a familiar face walked up to the counter to pay.

"How's it going?" Elsie asked.

"Busy." Ethan laughed, waving towards the line. "It's good to see you. How are you feeling after your crash?"

"I'm a little sore, but it's not bad. I wanted to say thanks to you and Lizzy for taking such good care of me."

"That storm was a bad one. I'm glad we were able to help."

Elsie nodded. "I heard Irma Mae is recovering as well. You guys were quite the team, rescuing everyone that crossed your path."

The flattery made Ethan uncomfortable. "Anyone would have helped in a similar situation."

"I'm not so sure about that." Elsie slid her credit card through the machine, smiling as she signed her name to the screen. "It doesn't matter anyway. You guys were the ones who did help. I felt bad about your shop not getting to open on time, so I made a post about it on the community page. Looks like people want a good love story."

"A what?" Ethan's ears felt broken, because it sounded a lot like Elsie had just referred to him and Lizzy as a love story.

"You know, like Romeo and Juliette. The shops are at war, but the owners can't keep their eyes off each other. The story practically wrote itself."

Ethan ran a hand across his forehead. "You know Lizzy was just teasing about us being boyfriend and girlfriend, right?"

"Of course." Elsie nodded, but then she gave a wink. "Sometimes it's not what a person says, but how they act that matters. I could see right through your charade. You guys are crazy about each other."

Ethan glanced across the street, wishing that Lizzy would appear out of thin air to help back him up. "I, we, uh." There weren't any words to say. He took a deep breath. "What else did you say in this post?"

"Oh, nothing much. I may have mentioned that both of

you happen to be incredibly talented bakers, and that you guys deserved the support of the town."

Ethan's mind was racing. He wanted to ask Elsie to take the article down, but it was too late. The customers had already come. Gratitude pushed to the top of his emotions.

"Thanks for helping this to be an incredible grand opening. I thought it was going to be a bust."

Elsie grinned. "If the crowd outside is any indicator, I think you'll be doing just fine for the next few days. Good luck."

She reached for her box of cookies and stepped to the side so Ethan could ring up the next customer. He was working on autopilot while his mind raced. It was incredible that people were coming into his store, but was it really all because of the story Elsie had told? It wouldn't hurt to ask around and see.

He cleared his throat and looked at the face of his next customer. "Welcome to Ethan's Crumbs. How did you hear about the shop?" The woman he was asking had two young children with her. They pointed excitedly at the cookies on the display tray.

"I read about your story while scrolling social media. I couldn't believe your grand opening got snowed out. The weather here can be so unpredictable at times."

Ethan nodded. "I agree. I'm not used to that kind of snow."

"I know. I read about how you guys saved dozens and

dozens of people from car crashes." She sighed. "It was heroic."

The next customer was up before he could correct her. Throughout the day, he heard different variations of Elsie's story. He was dying to check out the post, but the stream of customers wasn't slowing.

They were running out of cookies by mid-afternoon. Ethan finally taped a note to the door apologizing for closing early and inviting the customers to come back the next day. He locked the door and turned to his employees. They hadn't slowed down all day.

"How are you guys holding up?"

Chad swung his arms from side to side, loosening up his muscles. "That was nuts. Please tell me every day won't be like this."

As much as Ethan loved the idea of a busy shop, this had been too much. He couldn't imagine dealing with that many people every single day. "I sincerely hope not. If it is, I'm going to have to hire a few more employees."

Kim stepped into the lobby with a washcloth and began to spray down the tables. "It sure made the day fly by."

"That's true." Chad tossed spatulas and frosting bags into the giant mixing bowl, which he balanced on a stack of trays. He headed to the back and dumped them in the industrial sinks, turning on the faucet.

Kitty approached Ethan's side, lowering her voice. "So, when did you start dating Lizzy? I'm not sure if I should be scandalized that you're dating the competition or be impressed at your brilliant business move."

"You read the article?" Ethan pressed a button to print out the day's receipts and turned to Kitty.

"Yeah. I saw it during my break."

"Can you show me where it is?" Ethan held his phone out. When Kitty handed it back, Ethan's heart dropped. There was a post on the community page spinning the story way out of proportion.

According to Elsie, Ethan and Lizzy donned superhero capes and went about the city, looking for people to serve. Instead of a tragic backstory about the hero, the snow was the villain. From reading the story, it sounded like Elsie's car had been moments away from exploding, and that all the other people who came in narrowly escaped with their lives as well.

The love story that Elsie painted was a fabulous work of fiction, with details of all their interactions. According to the post, Ethan constantly snuck kisses when he didn't think anyone was watching. Lizzy followed him with her eyes everywhere he walked, like she couldn't stand to be away from him for more than a minute.

By the end of the post, Ethan and Lizzy were painted as star-crossed lovers who were determined to make their shops thrive, no matter how bad the opposition got. There was a plea from Elsie to not let these shops go down without a fight.

Kitty's eyes were trained on Ethan's when he finished reading. "So, is any of it true?"

It was a lot to digest. Ethan ran a hand through his hair with a sigh. "Parts of it, for sure. You know we were closed for the storm, and Lizzy and I did help a few people out, but this is so wildly exaggerated, I'm not sure what to say. I love the support, but how do I fix things without making Elsie sound like a liar?"

Kitty shook her head. "That's above my paygrade. I think you should probably talk to Lizzy."

"You're right. But first, let's get ready for tomorrow."

He pretended not to hear the sigh that escaped from Kitty's mouth. "I hope it isn't quite so busy."

"Me too." Ethan stayed in the shop long after the employees left. He had been planning on sending them home earlier, but they had all offered to stay until everything was cleaned up.

With silence in the shop, Ethan's mind spun in circles. He needed to say something about the article, but he had no clue what. It was going to be awkward bringing it up with Lizzy, but he was pretty sure she had already seen the post. Maybe she'd have some ideas.

Ethan gave the shop a final once over before he shut off the lights. There was a mix of nerves when he glanced towards Lizzy's shop. It was time to face the music. He walked out the front door, tugging the front of his jacket tight while he pulled the door shut behind him.

He was locking the door when he noticed a commotion down the street. Two men staggered down the sidewalk, laughing loudly while they passed a bottle back and forth. It was clear they had been drinking for a while. They came to a stop outside Lizzy's shop. He watched as they peered in the window and then stepped back, pointing to someone inside.

Ethan's stomach began to churn. It wasn't his problem who loitered on the sidewalk. It was public property. But Lizzy usually worked late, and she often walked out of her shop alone. The fact that Ethan knew Lizzy's habits coming and going meant he'd been watching her a little more than he liked. It also meant he was about to get a scolding for interfering because he wasn't about to leave her in potential danger.

The pit in Ethan's stomach grew. He walked across the street, heading right towards the men. As he walked, he calculated the best way to talk to them. The last thing he wanted was a fight on his hands.

The men stopped laughing as he approached, stepping towards him. "Hey man, what's up?"

"Nothing much," Ethan said. "I'm just here to pick up my girlfriend." The words rolled off his tongue. He reached for the doorknob, relieved to find that it was locked. At least Lizzy had that much common sense.

"That woman in there is your girlfriend?" the man with a mustache said. "She's hot."

Ethan grimaced. He needed to get the men away from the shop before Lizzy got hurt. "Yep. She's definitely pretty. But she's not available, guys."

The men shook their heads, as if trying to process what Ethan was saying. "So, if she's your woman, why aren't you going in to see her?"

Ethan held back a groan, clearly caught in his lie. "I, uh, forgot my key."

The shorter of the men pushed close to Ethan. "Or you don't really know this woman at all."

"Which means I've got a chance," the taller man said. He held his hand out for the bottle, taking a long swig before he turned his attention to Ethan. The alcohol on his breath was nauseating when he reached for Ethan's arm. "You wouldn't mess up my chance with the pretty lady, would you?"

Ethan's mind was spinning. He needed Lizzy to let him in, and he needed her to act naturally about it if the men were going to leave. Otherwise, there wasn't a chance in the world he was going to be able to keep either of them safe.

CHAPTER 11

❄

*L*izzy was elbow deep in soap suds, taking care of the final dishes for the day. The upside of owning a cookie shop was that all her dishes stacked nicely in one corner. Cookie sheets were made to nestle together, which made space saving much easier. The downside was the number of dishes she had to wash each night as each of those cookie trays got used.

She was scrubbing down one of the trays when a commotion outside caught her attention. A quick glance showed her the tuft of brown hair that she'd recognize anywhere. The sight of Ethan standing outside her shop caused her heart to kick up a few notches. Why did the most handsome man she'd ever talked to have to cause such complicated feelings? More importantly, what was he doing outside her shop?

Lizzy turned her head back towards the job at hand. If he wanted to hang around with buddies, couldn't he do it somewhere else? She figured he was probably pointing out the competition to his friends. Maybe their truce during the blizzard had been a temporary situation, but it had felt genuine.

She rinsed off the tray and stacked it on the drying rack with the other trays. The suds were draining down the sink when she heard a loud thud. Ethan was pressed against the window, being held in place by the two men she had assumed were his friends. The look on Ethan's face told a different story.

Lizzy discretely reached for the can of pepper spray she kept under the counter and walked towards the door. She turned the lock and swung the door open, holding the can out of sight.

"Can I help you guys?" she asked, trying to keep the trembling out of her voice.

"This guy says he's your boyfriend." The man who spoke had a ripped jacket and mud splattered jeans. He didn't look like he had showered in days.

"Yeah, but he doesn't seem to know how to get in your shop." The stench of alcohol and unwashed bodies wafted towards her. Ethan's eyes were pleading with her to help.

Lizzy pressed her hand against the door frame for support, trying to think fast on her feet. "Did you forget your key again?" she asked, keeping the tone of her voice light.

Ethan struggled against the men, shaking them off with a huff. "I think I left it at home." He leveled a glare at them that made them back up a step. "See? I told you I knew her."

One of the men held out his hand. "We're sorry, man."

The situation seemed to be deescalating, but Lizzy wasn't going to feel safe until Ethan was inside the shop with her, and the door was locked behind them.

"Did you need anything else, or can I have my boyfriend back?" Lizzy stared down the men, ready to spring into action with her pepper spray if they didn't leave.

"Nah, man. It's all a misunderstanding." The smaller man gave Ethan a rough shove towards Lizzy. Ethan stumbled forward, catching himself just a foot away from where Lizzy stood.

"Let's go inside," she said. She wasn't sure what, exactly, the situation outside had been, or why Ethan would tell anyone they were dating, but the situation felt tense. It was better to get them behind a locked door before she demanded answers.

Ethan nodded, and for the second time that week, he stepped into her cookie shop. The men stayed outside, watching their every move.

"Why do they think you're my boyfriend?" Lizzy asked. She worked hard to school her expression, so it looked like she was actually in love.

"I'll explain in a minute. Please don't hate me, but I think I have to hug you if we are going to get them to go away."

Lizzy gulped, every part of her body screaming that she

couldn't get close to the man who was tempting her to break her carefully thought-out plans. Career first. Then dating. Before she could overthink the situation, he was wrapping his arms around her. A jolt raced through her body as she sank into the hug.

He smelled incredible. Most guys smelled like cedar and pine trees and manly sorts of scents, but Ethan had a strong scent of spices. The hint of cinnamon blended with his cologne in an intoxicating way that made her reluctant to leave his grasp.

She had noticed his body before, but it was a different story to be held in his arms. If the chest she was pressed against was any indication, either he worked out frequently or God had gifted him with a perfect body. Either way, her cheek was certainly not disappointed to be pressing against his sculpted chest.

He was holding her close, but even as he did, his arms were loosely wrapped around her. This wasn't the hug of a boyfriend, but rather the hug of someone trying to respect her boundaries. For some reason, that was incredibly endearing.

"I'm so sorry about this," he murmured. The lilt of his voice, with heartfelt apology, was sending waves of desire through her body.

Lizzy was going to have a stern lecture with her heart later about responding inappropriately to hugs from her competitor, but it didn't feel like the right time. Instead, she slid her hands to the back of his shoulders, telling herself that it was necessary to help sell the story.

"I assume you're going to explain what is going on at some point, right?" Lizzy asked. Eventually he was going to let go, but she was rather comfortable where she stood. They gently swayed from side to side.

Ethan nodded. "It's simple. The guys were hanging around your store window, and they looked like they weren't up to any good. I came over to check it out, and they confirmed my suspicions."

A chill ran down Lizzy's spine. "They were waiting for me?"

"Yeah. And I stupidly told them we were dating. It made sense after the post today. I thought they'd back off if they knew you were taken, but it doesn't seem to matter." He reached for a strand of her hair, pushing it off her shoulders.

The men were watching the couple through the window, leering at Lizzy in a way that told her Ethan wasn't making anything up.

Lizzy gulped, trying to sort through his explanation. "I'm guessing they aren't buying the whole bit about us dating. They don't seem in any hurry to leave." She ran through her options in her mind. She could call the police, but all that would accomplish would be an officer asking the men to move along. There was no guarantee they wouldn't come back the moment the officer left.

She could sneak out the back door, but her car was parked out front, less than ten feet from where the men stood. Sneaking out wasn't going to help unless she wanted to walk home.

She could take her chances with the men. They gave off the air of men who had indulged a little too freely at the bar. With any luck, they were just in a flirty mood, and she'd be able to talk her way out of the mess. The thought of talking to them sent a shiver through her body. They didn't seem like men who'd appreciate being brushed off.

The easiest option would be to sell the story. "Do you trust me?" Lizzy asked, peering up at Ethan's face.

That earned a low chuckle that reverberated through her body. "Do I have a choice?"

Lizzy slid her hands to cup the back of his neck, telling herself that the electricity shooting through her body was an adrenaline rush that had nothing to do with the handsome man in front of her. She stood on her tiptoes and, kicking one foot up behind her like every other smitten woman in the movies, she pressed her lips to his.

Ethan's lips were pressed in a thin line, but they quickly softened as he began kissing her back. The electricity in her body was reaching critical mass. Every part of her mind was shouting at her to back down and take her chances with the men outside, but her heart was pushing her forward, urging her to make the kiss believable. The heart won.

Lizzy's breathing was ragged when she stepped back, seconds later. She snuck a glance past Ethan's shoulder, watching as the men outside elbowed one another before walking away.

"They're leaving," she said. She stepped back, rubbing

her hands down her jeans as if kissing Ethan was something she did every day.

"That was . . . unexpected," Ethan said. He straightened his shirt and tilted his head from side to side, cracking his neck.

"Sorry." Mortification was flooding through Lizzy's body, chasing away any lingering butterflies as she realized what she had done. "They didn't look like they were going to leave otherwise."

"I get that. It looks like your unconventional methods worked." Ethan's crystal blue eyes studied her face, the intensity startling. "I'm glad."

Lizzy's knees wobbled. She sank into a chair, the fear of the past few minutes catching up with her. The room started spinning and Lizzy leaned forward, resting her chin on clasped hands.

"Thank you for saving me." Lizzy looked at Ethan, who was staring out the window.

"You could have ignored the situation."

A dark shadow crossed Ethan's face as he clenched his fists. "This isn't the first time I've been in a situation like this."

"A girlfriend?" Lizzy guessed.

Ethan shook his head. "My other sister, Piper. She was fifteen, and things could have gone really badly for her if me and my friends hadn't shown up when we did."

Lizzy's heart sank, imagining the terror his sister must have felt. "Was she okay?"

His eyes were turned away when Ethan answered.

"Physically, yes. Emotionally, it took a while for her to trust going out with friends again. She lost faith in the world that night."

Lizzy watched Ethan's face as the shadows lifted. He turned to her, the crooked smile back on his face. "Do you know that she single-handedly was responsible for starting a program that dealt with teenage drinking? They now present that program in schools throughout the city so that more teens are aware of the consequences their actions can have. It is a lot easier to understand the seriousness of the situation when you are sober, sitting in a classroom."

"She sounds incredible." Lizzy thought about how she'd feel if she was in the same situation. "I'm glad you were there for her that night, and I'm grateful you were here tonight for me."

"Well, if we're being honest, you were there for me first. I'm guessing I'd be sporting a gnarly black eye if you hadn't opened the door."

Lizzy laughed. "You were pretty difficult to ignore, pressed against my store window like that." The tension from the evening was ebbing, leaving Lizzy completely drained. She glanced around the store. There were a few odds and ends she had planned to take care of before heading home, but they would have to wait until morning.

As she looked around, she remembered that Ethan had mentioned a post. "What did you mean when you said it made sense that they'd believe we were dating? What post are you talking about?"

"That's what I was coming to talk to you about. Was

your shop busy today?" Ethan's question felt like he was prying, but the tone of his voice held no accusations.

"It was. And honestly, I felt kind of bad. I was hoping you'd have most of the customers for your opening day."

"That's the thing. We were so busy, we ran out of cookies. I think most of it is because of Elsie's post she made on the community page." Ethan rubbed a hand down his arm. "I'm guessing you haven't read it yet."

Lizzy shook her head. "I think you'd better show me it, although I'm not sure I want to see what she wrote."

"That's probably a good choice." Ethan's eyes were sparkling when he pulled out a chair and sank down beside her. He pulled up the community page and held his phone out.

Scanning the first few sentences gave Lizzy a good idea of what was coming. Elsie had a knack for flowery language and extreme exaggeration. The parts about them being star-crossed lovers were especially interesting.

When she finished reading, she looked up. "Wow. I had no idea we were that awesome." Her tone was sarcastic, but Ethan's face fell.

"We can't let the town believe the things she said, can we? It feels so dishonest, somehow."

"Which part? The part where we're secretly dating or the part where we saved dozens of people from near death?" Lizzy's laughter was high pitched. "I get that her heart was in the right place, but this is madness."

Ethan ran a hand through his hair. "The crazy thing is

that I think she believes it. She told me she saw the chemistry between us. We are denying our true feelings."

He laughed, but Lizzy's lips were still tingling from their kiss. She wouldn't say she was in love with Ethan, but sparks were definitely there. As much as she hated to admit it, she was interested in getting to know him better.

"Any ideas on how to set the record straight without offending the entire town?" Lizzy's shop had been busy, but if it was all because of a fake article, that felt wrong.

"I was thinking we could comment, thanking her for her kind words while correcting some of the misconceptions."

"How would we do that without making her feel bad?"

Ethan cleared his throat. "How about this? We appreciate your glowing review. People all over the city worked hard the day of the blizzard to make sure neighbors were accounted for. We were happy to do our small part to help with a few fender benders. The real heroes were the first responders." Ethan fiddled with a fake flower in the center of the table. "Does that sound too defensive?"

"I like it. It addresses the car wrecks." Her mouth was dry. "What about us?"

Ethan pinned her down with his crystal blue eyes. "I see two solutions. We either admit that we are friendly competitors, or we try to date for real. I think we both know that dating isn't a good idea right now."

The thought of a relationship with Ethan sent a wave of longing through Lizzy's body. As much as she hated to admit it, she hadn't minded kissing him. In fact, it had been nice.

She swallowed once, trying to form the right words. "You're right. Let's set the public straight and admit that we are just friends."

A small frown pulled Ethan's lips down. "I do want to get to know you better, though. I just don't want the public to have their eyes on us."

"We'll see." Lizzy needed to steer the conversation back to safer territory. "Thanks again for your help. I imagine you were probably heading home when you noticed the men?"

The impish grin was back. "I was on my way to talk to you, but I really should be getting back. Cindy is waiting at home, and we have a hockey game to watch."

He was a hockey fan. The idea of him having other interests outside of his cookie shop shouldn't have been surprising, but it was. Lizzy realized she really knew very little about Ethan except that he had nice hair and a charming grin and two sisters. Then his words registered properly.

"You have a girlfriend waiting at home? I wouldn't have kissed you, even for pretend, if I knew you were dating someone." Lizzy felt awful. Maybe she had been really misreading Ethan's signals. Hadn't he asked her out? If he was two timing a girlfriend at home, Lizzy was going to be furious.

The dimple in his cheek appeared when he turned to

face her. "Cindy is my pet beagle, and I think she'll forgive you."

"So, no girlfriend?" The answer shouldn't matter because Lizzy couldn't be interested in the man beside her. Still, her heart had fluttered when he said he wanted to get to know her better.

"I moved here after my last breakup. I was tired of the big city life and the heartache that came with it."

"How long ago did that relationship end?" Lizzy was being nosy, but she couldn't keep the questions from coming. If she was honest, she wanted to know more about the man who smelled like the holidays. Even if he was her competition.

"Three months ago. We didn't date very long, but I was ready for a clean start. What about you? Do you have a boyfriend?" Ethan's eyes were searching hers, waiting for an answer.

"Nope. I have a plan. Career first, then marriage, then kids. A boyfriend doesn't fit into that scenario until my shop is up and running."

Ethan stood, pushing his chair back against the wall with a reluctant smile. "That sounds like a solid plan." He pulled a set of keys out of his pocket. "Are you okay here? I really should be getting home. The game is starting soon and Cindy hates to miss the face off."

Lizzy stood to follow Ethan. She held her hand out when they reached the door. "Enjoy the game. I hope your team wins."

Ethan shook her hand, their relationship professional

once again. As Lizzy locked the door behind him, she told her heart to settle down. One chivalrous act didn't make Ethan her friend. He was still her business rival, no matter how much she may have enjoyed their kiss.

She tried to shake the memory of his lips out of her mind. He was a distraction that could ruin everything she worked for. The percentages for a new business to take off were already slim enough without direct competition across the street.

More than ever, Lizzy was determined to make her dreams a reality. She had worked too long to get to this point. Her store was going to be around for the long haul, and if that meant driving Ethan's store out of business, she was going to have to stand firm.

With her determined attitude, she couldn't understand why her heart skipped a beat when she walked out of the shop, locking the door behind her. The blue awning across the way reminded her too much of the man who was trying to follow his dreams as well. If she was going to succeed, he was going to have to fail.

Somehow, that victory didn't sound so sweet.

CHAPTER 12

❄

*E*than's sleep was restless, with Lizzy's face featuring heavily in his dreams. Seeing her in danger had awakened memories that Ethan would rather forget. Was it really so difficult for men to treat women with respect? He understood the feeling of desire for a woman. He just didn't understand why people couldn't respect boundaries.

Waking up early to open the shop was a challenge after the non-stop rush the day before. Chad and Kitty were saints for sticking with him. They had been prepared for a normal morning, and not a crowd.

He was curious what the reception would be today. Lizzy had helped Ethan to write a kind but firm post thanking their customers for the support. They had posted it to the community page late last night. The hope was to counter Elsie's helpful but exaggerated post from the day before.

Ethan pulled out his phone and scrolled to his post, looking for any comments he could answer. The first dozen were customers raving about the cookies. A picture stopped his scrolling. The photo was taken from outside the shop, with the two drunk men looking in at what was clearly Lizzy and Ethan sharing an intimate moment.

The caption was simple. **"Just friends" looks different from where I'm standing.**

It was one comment in a sea of others, but it was all it took to derail the rest of the thread. Now, instead of fixing the rumors, someone had added fuel to the flames.

Ethan studied the picture. He took in Lizzy's bright eyes and parted lips, inches away from his. She looked like she cared about him, even though it had all been an act.

Kissing her had probably been a bad idea, but he didn't know what else they could have done. He wouldn't mind kissing her again, but her boundaries had been very clear. He needed to head to work and put all distractions out of his mind.

A cold frost had gripped the town during the night. Ethan scraped ice off his car, grateful for the heavy gloves he wore. The heater was barely kicking on by the time he reached Main Street.

The store fronts were all dark except for Lizzy's shop, which shone like a welcoming beacon in the dark night. He could see her walking back and forth, her hair pulled back from her face while she stirred something in a large bowl.

Ethan pulled his car around to the back parking lot,

turning his attention to the tasks for the day. The grand opening had been a resounding success, but the large number of people visiting the store had also been a wakeup call. They needed to streamline how they worked if they wanted to help customers more efficiently.

Chad showed up a couple hours later, stomping snow off his boots when Ethan opened the door to let him in. He glanced over Chad's head towards Lizzy's shop. She was watching them out the window. When Ethan lifted his hand to wave, she ducked behind the counter.

That was odd behavior, but Ethan shook it off. He looked at Chad. "I'm glad you came back today. Yesterday was intense."

Chad shook his head back and forth, snowflakes flying off his hair before he stepped inside. "I figured it was probably a one-day thing. I'm seriously hoping most days aren't that bad."

"Me too." Ethan looked out the window while Chad hung up his coat in the back. Lizzy was setting a new box of cookies in her display window. This time, when she caught his eye, she gave a little wave. He was waving back when Chad came into the room.

"Are you guys flirting again?"

Ethan turned slowly to face him. "Why would you say that?"

Chad shrugged. "It's the post you guys made. I didn't realize you were secretly dating."

"We're not." It was a struggle to keep the emotion out of

his voice. "There was an incident last night with some drunk guys. I had to pretend like I was dating Lizzy to get them to go away."

"Hey, man. You don't have to give me any excuses. I think you guys look good together." Chad slipped an apron over his head, wrapping the strings around his back before tying the apron in the front. "What are we working on today?"

Ethan's emotions were bubbling near the surface while he worked. He pointed to a stack of frosting bags. "You can get to work on the frostings. I'll start the first batch of dough."

The industrial stand mixer on the floor provided enough noise to drown out Ethan's thoughts. He creamed butter, adding sugar until it was fluffy. As ingredients were added, the dough began to come together.

Once the cookies were in the oven, it took just a few minutes for the aroma to fill the shop. Ethan stood straight, breathing the scent of fresh baked cookies. This always grounded him and reminded him of the goals he was working towards.

Ten minutes before opening, he slid the final tray into a warming oven. Most of the cookies were served cold, but the chocolate chip cookies were always hot.

Kitty and Sarah arrived as Ethan was flipping the sign to say open.

"What do you think today is going to be like?" Sarah asked.

Ethan shrugged. "Your guess is as good as mine. I was shocked to see so many people yesterday."

"That's probably because you and Lizzy make such a cute couple," Kitty teased.

Ethan's head slumped forward while he sighed. "Why can't people believe we are friends? And new friends, at that?"

Kitty's phone was in her hand, and she held up the picture that Ethan hoped to never see again. "You can't fake the expression on her face. She's clearly smitten. And you're holding her in a way that suggests much more than friends."

Chad straightened his apron before walking to the front of the store. He headed to Kitty's side. "Ethan claims that they were showing off for the guys outside the window. I didn't fully get it, but he had some excuse about them pretending to be a couple so the guys would leave."

Ethan flicked a towel in Chad's direction. "You're the worst." The problem was that the way Chad described things, the lowlife scum sounded more like part of a joke than the actual truth. Ethan guessed that this was just one of many photos that were taken. The angles were too perfect for it to be a candid shot.

As much as he hated to admit it, this picture wasn't just about him. There were two parties that were being affected. After a small flurry of customers, Ethan wiped down the countertops. He waited a few minutes to make sure no one else was coming in, and then he cleared his throat.

"You guys okay here while I head out for a quick errand?"

Chad nodded like it was no big deal, but Sarah wasn't nearly as subtle.

"Tell Lizzy we say hi." She was trying not to laugh.

Ethan left the store with his employees joking behind his back. He was going to have to find a solution to the gossip or constantly worry that people were talking about him.

Lizzy looked up when Ethan stepped through the door. She met his eyes, and his stomach did a little flip that he was beginning to associate with being around her. She made him nervous in the best sort of way.

Ethan waited while Lizzy rang up a customer. He hadn't been paying attention to the people in the room around him until the conversations in the store gradually dropped off. Ethan turned his head to the side, taking in the people in his peripheral vision. More than one customer was staring at his back, waiting, presumably, to see what Ethan was going to do.

So much for keeping the rumors down. As soon as Lizzy finished with the customer, Ethan stepped forward. "Can we talk somewhere private?" He spoke with a low voice, but Maria laughed quietly behind them.

"We'll take care of things out here," she said, waving Lizzy away.

The walk down the short hallway to Lizzy's small office took far longer than Ethan expected it would. He waited until they were tucked inside, and then he closed the door for privacy.

It had seemed like a good idea until he turned back to see Lizzy, standing inches from his face. She was close enough for him to smell the faint undertones of her floral perfume mixed with vanilla. Reaching forward to cup her face in his hands would be so easy. So would leaning in to kiss her soft lips.

"Hi," she said. She bit the side of her lip before looking away.

"Hi." Ethan wasn't sure what to do with his hands. He had enjoyed kissing Lizzy the night before, but she had been under duress. Standing in her tiny office made it difficult to focus on why he was there. "How are you feeling after last night?"

Lizzy's cheeks paled. "I think the adrenaline wore off once I got home. I couldn't stop shaking last night."

Ethan pulled her into a hug. "I'm so sorry. I should have done more."

"That's ridiculous." Lizzy snapped her eyes to his. "You were there when no one else was."

She gave a little shudder, and Ethan pressed her close. "I could have reported the guys. They should be rotting in a jail cell somewhere. Who knows who they will harass next?"

He couldn't help but feel guilty. What if someone else got hurt while he was flirting with Lizzy?

"Last I checked, the police don't really arrest people for walking down the sidewalk. Or for looking in public store windows." Lizzy slid her hand to Ethan's chest, covering his heart. "You can't save everyone, but you did help me. I'll always be grateful for that."

It would be easy to sway back and forth with Lizzy, sneaking in a couple of kisses, but that wasn't why Ethan came. He cleared his throat and stepped back.

"I'm not sure how much help I was. Did you read the responses to our post yet?"

Lizzy shook her head. "A couple of them. I slept in late, so I didn't have much time. How do they look?"

Ethan pulled up the picture and turned his phone so Lizzy could take it. He watched her face as she studied the photo, his heart aching when her face fell.

"Who took this picture?" Her jaw was tight.

"I don't know. They posted anonymously."

Lizzy took a step back, but there really wasn't anywhere for her to go. Ethan pressed his back against the door to give her room.

"I can't believe someone would stoop that low. Do you feel like everything is working against us to get our shops going?" Lizzy walked to the chair behind her desk and slumped down.

Ethan didn't like the unease that had settled between them, but he wasn't sure what to say. He was in the photo, too, but the attack felt more personal to Lizzy. He chose his words carefully. "Sometimes. I'm not sure why they posted the picture, but I also don't know what we can do about it. We can't exactly deny that it's the two of us together."

Lizzy's phone was out now, and she was scrolling through the comments. She stopped to lay the phone down on the desk. "The person who took this was on your side of the street. Do you know who it was?" There was a hint of accusation in the tone of her voice.

Her words took Ethan's breath away. "Are you suggesting that I had something to do with this?"

Instead of denying the question, Lizzy shrugged. "It doesn't look good to me."

Ethan's stomach began to roil. He reached for the door handle, the need for clear air pressing down on him.

"We don't know each other well, but I thought you knew me well enough to know that I'd never do anything like that." He shoved his hair back off his face. "Were you ever really interested in trying to be friends? Or was that just an act?"

He didn't give Lizzy time to answer. Before she could speak, Ethan was out the door and heading for the back exit. The last thing he needed was a room full of customers watching him storm out.

The wind hit Ethan's face with an icy blast when he stepped into the parking lot filled with piles of snow. He grunted and pulled his coat closed but the cold seeped through, bringing on a round of shivers. Ethan kicked at a snowbank, letting some of his frustration go.

He tried to see things from Lizzy's perspective, but he couldn't. It was one thing to keep her distance. They were competitors, after all. It was another to believe him capable

135

of posting those kinds of pictures. What would be the purpose of a smear campaign?

Ethan took the long way back to his store. He needed the walk to clear his mind so he could interact with his customers the way they deserved. There was no point worrying about any backlash the picture would have. He'd deal with the next problem when it came.

CHAPTER 13

❄

Thanksgiving Day couldn't come fast enough. It had been a week since the incriminating photo had been published, and yet Lizzy still heard comments about it every day. The town seemed more than happy to embrace the idea that the cookie shop owners were engaged in a super-secret romance. It was Lizzy who was struggling with the gossip.

"Maisy, it just isn't fair that I'm getting lumped into the same category as him. Every time I think I'm getting some good press, his name is mentioned, too. How am I supposed to stand out when everyone seems to think we're the same shop?"

Lizzy chatted with her sister while she drove four hours south to spend Thanksgiving weekend with her family in warmer weather. A healthy serving of her aunt Linda's famous rolls was the cure she needed. She couldn't wait to pull into the familiar driveway and walk up to the house that held so many memories.

Maisy's voice came across the speaker, and Lizzy realized her thoughts had drifted. "Sorry. What did you say?"

"I asked, why does it matter if people associate your shops with each other?"

"They'll feel like they can shop at either one." Lizzy passed a car in the fast lane who was driving the exact speed limit. The driver was doing his best to be a law-abiding citizen, but all it did was frustrate Lizzy. You shouldn't be in the fast lane unless you wanted to go fast.

"I don't get paid if someone goes to Ethan's shop. A lot of our flavors are different, but the staples are similar. I don't earn a dime when someone buys Ethan's chocolate chip cookies instead of mine."

"I'm sorry, sis. That sounds frustrating."

Maisy was saying the right words, but nothing was calming the storm that brewed in Lizzy's heart.

"What if my shop goes under because of him?"

Maisy coughed. "Impossible. You make the best designer sugar cookies anywhere in town. Your customers aren't going away."

The road narrowed to two lanes and traffic immediately slowed. Lizzy got stuck behind a big rig with a driver who was going fifty in a seventy mile per hour zone. Lizzy drummed her fingers on the steering wheel. She didn't have road rage, but she certainly understood why some people did. Everyone seemed determined to go slow today.

"I'm not worried about losing customers, exactly. I'm

more worried about losing the shop. It's so nice having a big space to work in instead of trying to run a business out of my home kitchen."

"I get that. You do have a pretty awesome set up."

Brake lights turned on in front of Lizzy, with cars skidding to a stop. "Hey sis, I'd better go. It looks like traffic is going to be gnarly for a minute."

"I'm excited to see you soon. You've got this. Kisses."

"Loves." Lizzy couldn't wait to see her sister if the traffic ever picked up again. The way things were looking, she'd get home by Christmas.

That was the last conversation Lizzy had with anyone for the rest of the drive. She took advantage of the stopped traffic to pull up her favorite playlist. With the windows rolled up, surrounded by strangers, Lizzy sang at the top of her lungs. She got a few sideways glances from the driver in the car next to her, but she didn't care. They'd never see her again.

Each mile that brought Lizzy closer to home gave her a sense of relief. She hadn't realized how wound up she had been until she pulled into the front of the garage and burst into tears. After quickly dabbing her eyes, Lizzy took a deep breath. She didn't need her mom to be asking questions.

There was no worry of that. Lizzy walked into a house that was a flurry of activity. The smell of fresh baked rolls permeated the air. Lizzy's mouth began to water. She dropped her bag by the front door and wandered through the house, surprised that her parents hadn't come to greet her yet.

Her aunt Linda was standing at the counter in the kitchen, covered with a fine misting of flour, but the smile on her face said that she didn't mind. She dropped the dough that she was working with back on the counter and came forward to press Lizzy into a giant hug.

"Hello, my beautiful niece. I missed you!"

The tension lifted from Lizzy's shoulders as she hugged her back. "Hi Linda. I missed you, too. Where's mom?"

"She ran to the store, but she should be back in just a few minutes. She's been talking nonstop about you coming home."

Linda walked back to the dough, which she continued to punch down. She pulled the dough away from the counter, stretching it into a line before she folded it back on itself. Linda's rolls were one of the biggest hits of Thanksgiving dinners. Lizzy knew that no snitching was allowed, but she decided to try her luck.

"It's been a long drive," she said, pulling her lips into a frown. "I'm starving."

"Let me guess. Are you by any chance hungry for fresh baked rolls?" Linda wasn't fooled by the act.

Lizzy grinned. "If you are offering, I won't say no. Just to be polite, of course."

"Of course." Linda handed Lizzy a giant roll before sliding butter and jam across the counter to her.

Lizzy tore off a corner of the roll and put it in her mouth, closing her eyes while she chewed. There was a reason why Linda's rolls were never left over after a meal. They were fluffy and buttery, melting in Lizzy's mouth.

She was taking another bite when her cousins, Aiden and Felix ran into the room. They skidded to a stop in front of her, their mouths dropping open.

"She gave you a roll?" Felix asked.

"I thought we had to wait until tomorrow," Aiden said.

Linda shooed their hands away with a smile. "When you drive four hours to visit your favorite aunt, then you can have your rolls early, too. Right now, you need to get out of my kitchen so I can make enough for tomorrow."

The boys ran off, laughing as they did so. They knew Linda liked to tease.

A comfortable silence settled on the kitchen, punctuated by the sound of the dough being kneaded.

"Do you need any help?" Lizzy knew what the answer would be, but she still wanted to offer.

Linda used the back of her arm to wipe her forehead. "I've got this."

For as long as Lizzy could remember, her aunt insisted on making the rolls on her own. The two days of cooking were worth it if she could keep the old family recipe a secret.

"You're the best." Lizzy hugged her aunt from behind. "Where's dad?"

"He's probably off tinkering with something in the garage. I can't keep track of my brother."

"I'll go hunting."

Lizzy left the kitchen, pausing in the family room to

take in the scene of chaos that was unfolding before her. Two of her brothers were laying on the floor under a pile of nieces and nephews. Shrieks and giggles pierced the air while the uncles struggled to free themselves from the pile.

"Who's winning?" Lizzy asked, standing by a chair.

"We are," the children yelled. They didn't bother to look at who was talking to them.

"Good luck," she told her brothers. They had both married young, but seeing the steadily growing pile of children that they were having made Lizzy feel behind, somehow. She couldn't help but feel a twinge of guilt that she wasn't ready for that kind of a commitment.

The garage door was askew when she approached, strengthening Linda's claim that her dad was probably inside working on something.

Lizzy found him standing in front of a contraption, wrench in hand.

"Hi, Dad," she called.

Her dad dropped the wrench and spun to see her, his entire face lighting up. "Lizzy! You got here faster than I expected."

As per usual, he was so absorbed in the project at hand, he hadn't paid any attention to the time. Instead of correcting him, Lizzy ran down three steps and buried her face in her dad's chest. His arms wrapped around her in a bear hug, and Lizzy finally felt like she was truly home.

She pulled back a second later. "What's the new project?"

"It's a turkey fryer. I got it at a garage sale."

"And you trust it enough to cook a turkey without exploding?" Lizzy had heard horror stories about turkey fryers gone wrong.

"Yeah. I'm just tightening the bolts for the handles on the outside. I got it from Mr. Green, and he wouldn't lie to me. Not about this."

Mr. Green had been their neighbor for years. If he said the contraption worked, it would be fine. "Alright. Just remember, I'm not making enough at the shop yet to cover all your medical bills if you drop the turkey on yourself instead of the platter."

Her dad laughed. "How is the shop going anyway?"

"It's exhausting. Remember how you guys kept telling me it would be hard work, and I kept telling you it would be fine?"

"I do." He smiled in a way that said he was waiting to hear that he had been right.

"Yeah. I should have listened. I was prepared for a long slog, but this has been far worse than I imagined."

"It probably doesn't help that you're spending your time flirting with the shop owner across the street."

Lizzy's jaw dropped. "Who has been gossiping about me here?"

Her dad ducked his head. "It may have been your mom, but I'll never reveal my sources."

Lizzy rolled her eyes. "I don't know why I thought you guys would miss that. I'm sure mom saw the post the day it was published."

"Yeah. She follows everything about your shop."

Maybe having her family in on the drama would be good. Lizzy could certainly use an outsider's perspective. She was handing a screwdriver to her dad when a car pulled into the driveway with a loud purr.

"That's your mom. You'd better go give her a hug."

"Thanks, Dad. Good luck with the fryer." She ran into the house and headed for the front door, pausing in the family room to call for reinforcements. "Who wants to help Grandma carry groceries in?"

Aiden and Felix jumped up. "We do." They ran to the front door while Lizzy followed slowly behind. She held the door open for them as they bounded down the steps, surrounding her mom with their chatter. Lizzy watched as her mom teased her grandsons before handing them each a bag.

"Hi, Mom," Lizzy called, stepping to the side while the twins ran back into the house with their treasures.

"You made it."

Lizzy held her composure until her mom wrapped her in a hug. Then the waterworks started.

"Shh. You're okay. I'm here." The words were soothing, but Lizzy had been holding in her emotions for too long. She let herself cry out the anger and frustration she had been feeling, knowing she was safe.

Instead of walking into the house, Lizzy's mom pulled her down to the steps.

"Do you want to tell me what's going on?"

Lizzy wiped her eyes. "It's the stupid gossip about the shop. Really, about me."

Mrs. Thompson rested her hand on Lizzy's shoulder. "I read about it. If I'm being honest, Ethan and you look cute together."

"Ugh." Lizzy picked a leaf off the porch and threw it. "We're not together. Not by a long shot. In fact, after the way I treated him last week, we're probably never speaking again."

"That sounds extreme."

Lizzy pulled out her phone and zoomed in on the photo from the post. She pointed to an orange streak she had found a few days before. It looked suspiciously like the fall leaves on display in Ethan's shop. "Someone across the street took this picture. It doesn't make any sense that it would be anyone other than Ethan."

"You mean the Ethan who is clearly holding you with a smitten expression on his face?"

"I know how it looks. He could have had someone else take the picture." Lizzy was tired of trying to justify her theories. "I don't know anyone else who would go to the lengths he did to get me to kiss him."

Mrs. Thompson's eyes shot up. "You kissed Ethan?"

Oops. Lizzy hadn't meant to share that. "Only because the guys outside wouldn't go away." She shuddered, remembering how tense she had felt in the situation. Ethan had acted so worried, it felt like they had no other choice except to act like they were dating.

"Why don't you tell me the whole story, starting with

how you came to be in his arms?" Mrs. Thompson grabbed a blanket off the porch chair and draped it over their laps.

Lizzy took a steadying breath before launching into the story. The entire encounter had lasted just a few minutes, but it had caused major ripples. As she spoke, Ethan's eyes kept flashing before her. If he had set the entire ruse up, then how did he seem so worried?

The longer Lizzy spoke, the more pieces began to click into place. He hadn't been the one to suggest the kiss. She had. He hadn't been the one to lean in first. She had. If anyone was manipulating that situation, it had been her.

Her mom didn't say anything until Lizzy fell silent. "You were almost attacked in front of your store." The statement conveyed all the horror a mom could feel.

A chill ran down Lizzy's spine, causing her to shiver. "Yeah."

"And Ethan saved you."

Lizzy wrapped her arms around her knees. In telling the story, she realized she had made a mistake. A huge one. Instead of being a friend, Lizzy had shoved Ethan's brave act in his face.

"Mom, I think I messed up."

"I can't say if you did or didn't, but I know there are very few things that can't be fixed with a good apology."

"It isn't going to happen." Lizzy shook her head. "Logically I know you're right, but I saw the look on his face. He doesn't want to talk to me ever again."

Aiden and Felix burst through the door, interrupting their conversation with their giggles.

"I think that's our cue." She rested a hand on Lizzy's arm. "You're good at taking care of problems. I have no doubt you'll figure this one out."

"Thanks, Mom."

Mrs. Thompson reached out to tickle Aiden while Lizzy hopped up to chase Felix inside. Being surrounded by unconditional love was exactly the cure Lizzy needed.***

Forcing herself to enjoy the Thanksgiving holiday was a stretch, but Lizzy tried to immerse herself in all the chaos her family had to offer. She'd worry about her shop when she got home. At least, that's what she tried to tell herself.

Physically, she was present for every meal. Mentally, her mind obsessed over the coming holiday season. Retailers would be pulling from her customer base while people scrambled to make sure they had all the gifts they needed. If they only had a few hours to run errands, she wanted to make sure they'd finish the day with a treat.

Lizzy was still mulling over how to talk to Ethan when she went home. They'd gotten hit on social media again. This time, it was a post comparing the stores side by side with a breakdown of the cookie flavors. According to the post, Lizzy had the best sugar cookies, but Ethan had the most creative new flavors. The anonymous author of the post speculated about if they worked out recipes together in their spare time.

She flung her phone down on the bed with a huff. When Maisy walked in a few minutes later, Lizzy was laying down beside the phone, still as a statue.

"You okay, sis?"

"Barely." Lizzy pulled herself up. "I can't wait to get back to the shop, but I'm also dreading seeing Ethan."

"Did you figure out what to say yet?" Maisy sat on the bed, her legs dangling off the side.

"Nope. Every time I think I've got it down, something changes. Like this." She showed the latest post to Maisy. "It's bad enough that everyone thinks we own the same shop. Now they are showing our stores side by side, so it is easy to compare the two."

Maisy studied the picture. As she did, her eyes widened. "Pull up the other post."

"Which one?"

"You know. The one with you two kissing."

Lizzy grabbed a throw pillow and swung it at her sister's back. Maisy dodged out of the way with a laugh. "I mean, the one with you looking deeply into his eyes while he protects you from the scary men outside."

"That's worse." Lizzy swatted her with the pillow again. "Who said you could come in my room anyway?"

"Um, we share a room, remember?" Maisy pointed to her half of the room.

"You've got me there." Lizzy pulled up the photo, handing her phone back to Maisy.

Maisy texted the photos to her phone.

"Why would you do that?" Her sister's behavior didn't make sense.

Maisy pulled up the picture of the couple on Lizzy's phone, zooming in to the orange streak. Then she pulled up her own phone, zooming in on Ethan's shop. "Do you notice anything strange?"

Lizzy looked back and forth between the photos, shaking her head. "Not really."

Maisy pointed to Ethan's storefront. "There's no bright orange in his display."

Once Maisy pointed it out, Lizzy couldn't look away. Remorse flooded her body, immediately followed by a guilt that weighed her down with the heaviness of what she had accused him of. Ethan had tried to be kind, and Lizzy had thrown it back in his face.

"Thanks, Maisy." She handed the phone back. "I don't know how I can come back from this one, but I'm going to try."

Maisy nodded. "You do realize that you have a bigger problem than Ethan, right?"

"What do you mean?" Lizzy wasn't ready for any more problems.

"Well, someone obviously took that picture. If it wasn't from Ethan's shop, then it would be one of the other shops on that side of the street. Someone was trying to sabotage you."

A new kind of heaviness filled Lizzy's body. All the other store owners had acted happy to have her move in. Was it all pretend? She was going to have to warn Ethan, but that would mean swallowing a lot of pride.

Lizzy prayed she wasn't too late.

CHAPTER 14

❄

*C*ars drove down Main Street, their windshield wipers furiously trying to remove the snow that drifted in sporadic flurries. Ethan was standing at the window, boxing up all the Thanksgiving decorations. He looked up occasionally to smile and wave as a car honked in passing, but he couldn't wait to get out of the spotlight.

He had come from a larger city, where people were too busy with their own lives to worry about anyone else's. Now he was smack dab in the center of small-town gossip. He hated the way it felt, like there was always someone watching every move to see if he was going to mess up.

Out of habit he glanced across the street. He had seen Lizzy's employees coming and going, but he hadn't seen her around for a few days. That was probably for the better since he didn't really have anything to say to her. He had used up all his politeness for the year.

Ethan let out a sigh of relief when every trace of fall decor was out of his windows. The city decorating contest started in a week, and he was going to need every spare minute to get his display up.

He had started designing his window the day he got his keys to the shop. Ethan had a fiercely competitive streak. Winning the contest didn't matter, but the grand prize certainly did. Lizzy's rude attitude had only added to his drive. He was going to show her which cookie shop was truly the best.

A small ding alerted him to a customer entering the shop, but he ignored it. Kitty was at the counter. She'd call him over if they got too busy. He pulled out a marker to label the fall boxes so he could pull them out again the following year, assuming the shop was still open.

That was negative thinking. Ethan replaced the thought with a vision of how the window would look. The winter wonderland he was creating was sure to win.

Ethan lifted the first of the boxes and turned, bumping into Lizzy. "Sorry." He said it out of habit, but he didn't really mean it. She had made it perfectly clear that she didn't want to be anywhere near him.

"It's my fault. I was in the way." Lizzy's eyes were sincere, but Ethan wasn't taking any chances. With no decorations in the window, the store was wide open for everyone to see them talking.

"As you can see, I've got my hands full. Kitty can take care of you." Ethan walked past Lizzy and headed through the store to the back exit, aware of the fact that she was trailing right behind him.

"Can we talk for a minute?"

Ethan unlocked his trunk and slid the box in as far back as it would go. "I think we've said all there is to say, Lizzy. I'm not in the mood for another post about us to hit the community page." He pulled the door open, heading inside for another box.

Lizzy reached for his arm, pulling him to a stop. "That's what this is about."

Ethan glanced at the front of the store, where Kitty was engaged in a conversation with a customer. He had a few minutes, but he wasn't sure he wanted to hear anything Lizzy had to say.

"Please. I'll be quick."

"Fine." Ethan walked into his office, heading around the desk so he could sit as far away from Lizzy as possible. He didn't need a repeat of the feelings that coursed through his body last time he was in a closed room with her.

He pushed back from the desk, regarding her with mistrust. "What do you need?"

Lizzy pulled out her phone. "For starters, I need to apologize. The last time we spoke I wasn't kind. I was frustrated and scared, but that didn't give me any right to treat you that way."

An apology wasn't what Ethan expected to hear. If Lizzy was going to play nice, he could take time to listen to the rest of what she had to say. He waved his hand towards the folding chair on the other side of the desk. "You can sit, if you want."

"Thanks." Lizzy pulled out her phone, turning it over in her hands.

"What made you change your mind?" Ethan was happy she was being nice, but he didn't trust it.

"There were a few things. For starters, I remembered how you treated me when the guys were outside. I'm guessing that if you were really trying for a photo op, you would have initiated the kiss. And you wouldn't have broken it off." She looked down at her hands before meeting his eyes. "You were a gentleman that day."

"I didn't have a choice." Ethan flipped the edge of a pad on his desk, repeatedly, the pages falling against each other.

"You're wrong. You had a choice, and you used it to make sure I was comfortable and felt safe. I let myself forget that when you came to talk to me."

Ethan nodded. "I promised I didn't set you up, and I meant it."

"I know." Lizzy pulled out her phone. "I believe you, but I can also prove it."

Ethan's heart began to thump against his ribcage. If Lizzy had proof of who was tormenting them, then they could stop the rumors.

She held out the photo of them embracing. "I know you remember this picture far better than you ever wanted to, but see that streak of orange in the corner? It's important."

Ethan gave a brief nod, not trusting himself to speak.

He looked down as Lizzy swiped to a different photo. She held it out and his breath caught in his throat.

"This is your shop."

Ethan nodded. He had seen it before. "Yep. It's my shop. Why does it matter?"

Lizzy flipped back to the first photo. "That orange streak is part of a fall leaf. It can't have come from your shop. The colors are all wrong."

Ethan's mind swirled. He hadn't paid much attention to the photo, but Lizzy's observation was spot on. That meant someone across the street really had been snapping photos of them. But why? What did they hope to accomplish?

"I never noticed that. I told you that I was innocent when I came to your shop."

"And I stubbornly ignored what you said."

Ethan ran a hand through his hair. "I'm more confused than ever. I don't understand why they'd go to all that trouble to post a picture like that."

"I agree. I'm not sure why they'd do it, but I know it wasn't you."

The entire situation was making Ethan's head throb. "It's already been posted. Can we just move on?"

Lizzy shook her head. "That's the problem. I don't think we can. Someone took the photo when we were in a vulnerable spot."

"They didn't know that."

"Maybe not, but posting it in the first place sure feels deliberate." Lizzy leaned her elbows on the table. "I think someone is trying to sabotage both of us."

Her words filled the air planting tendrils of doubt in Ethan's mind. "Why would anyone want to hurt us?"

That was the crux of the situation. Figuring out why someone wanted them to close would be almost impossible to find. It was much easier to blame each other.

Lizzy crossed her leg, bouncing one foot while her mouth turned down. "I don't know why they'd be trying to hurt us, but I have an idea for how to catch them."

"I'm all ears." Ethan sat straight in his chair, clasping his hands on the table.

"Well, I have two thoughts. The first is to get photos of the shop windows before they take their decorations down. It should be easy to spot which stores have a clear shot into mine."

Ethan shook his head. "It's too late. They were taking down their displays today, too. I think everyone is trying to get their Christmas windows ready, so the city doesn't fine them."

Lizzy pulled a strand of hair forward, twisting it around her finger. "That doesn't work so well."

"Nope." Ethan was trying to pay attention, but he was getting the tingles again that reminded him he was a little too interested in Lizzy's hair. They needed to leave the office before he forgot why he couldn't reach out to brush it back.

He cleared his throat. "You said you had a couple of ideas. What's the other one?"

Lizzy ducked her head. "It's so embarrassing."

Ethan smiled. He was the one that would be embarrassed if Lizzy could read his thoughts.

"I promise I'll only laugh a little bit."

"Thanks." She rolled her eyes, and Ethan's stomach did a little flip. The lines were so much easier to keep straight when she was angry with him. Now they were dangerously close to crossing into flirting territory.

She ran her hands down her jeans. "What if we try to catch them in the act?"

"I don't see how that would work. How can we catch them if they are only interested in us?" Ethan trailed off as he caught the gist of what she was asking. "Oh. We'd be the bait."

Lizzy covered her face with her hands, peeking out at him between her fingers. "Is that awful to suggest?"

It was difficult to form a response because if he understood what Lizzy was suggesting, she was asking him to spend time near her. They would be feeding the public the very relationship they had been denying since Elsie's post.

Lizzy mistook his hesitation for a no. "Never mind. It's a crazy idea."

Ethan reached out to cover her hand with his. "It's crazy for sure, but what if it works?" He tried not to focus on how soft her skin felt, or the fact that he may be holding that hand for real before long.

"It would tell us who was behind the smear campaign . . ."

"And hopefully let us figure out why. I'm in." Ethan realized that he was still holding Lizzy's hand. He casually slid his back to the notepad he had been playing with. "Any ideas on how to start?"

Lizzy jerked her head towards the door. "How much do you trust Kitty and Chad?"

"They're both good kids. Why?"

"Well, if we're the bait, we can't exactly see who is watching us. We're going to need help."

The idea of Kitty creeping into a store like a spy lifted the corners of his mouth. She'd stand out immediately. "I'm sure they'd both be happy to help, although I'm not sure how much help they would actually be."

It was Lizzy's turn to reach across the table for his hand. "As our first official spy act, let's meet tonight after the shops close. How do you feel about leaving work and then driving around the block to come into the back of my store? I think we can all fit in the kitchen to discuss plans out of the sight of anyone passing by."

Ethan's hand tingled from her touch. "I'm in."

"It's a date." Lizzy stood, pushing the folding chair into place. "Don't forget to invite Kitty and Chad as well."

"I'll let them know." Ethan held the door open for Lizzy, waiting until he heard the bell chime over the door before he headed back to the window. It was difficult to focus when he had a spy mission to plan, but the decorating contest needed to be foremost on his mind. Once his display was built, it was going to be difficult for anyone to sneak a picture of him unawares.

* * *

THREE DAYS later it was time to spring the plan. Ethan watched out the window, waiting for Lizzy's signal. She stood in front of her store window and yawned, stretching her hands high above her head. Ethan waited for her to lower her arms. Then he reached for his jacket and headed outside, leaving Sarah and Kim in charge.

He "bumped" into Lizzy while walking down the street. "I'm so sorry," he said, raising his voice louder than usual. "I didn't see you."

"I'm the one who is sorry. I'll watch where I'm going next time."

It was hard to keep a straight face, but as Ethan expected, a few people were already paying attention to the couple. "Where are you headed?" Ethan asked.

"I was going window shopping to look for a gift for my mom." Lizzy held her hand out. "Do you want to come with me?"

Ethan took her hand, grateful for the gloves they wore. Pretending to have a relationship with Lizzy was far easier to do when he wasn't touching her skin. He gave her hand a squeeze while they meandered across the street.

"You're doing great," Lizzy whispered. She pulled him to the first window, oohing and aahing over the decorations in the scooter shop. "Look. Gingerbread people." The window display held a small table with Mr. and Mrs. Clause on either end. There was a stack of gingerbread cookies on the table between them.

Ethan waved through the window at the shop owners, making sure they saw them.

"Have you considered having gingerbread for one of your weekly flavors?" Ethan could imagine how cute Lizzy would decorate each person.

"Maybe. I'm not sure it's worth my time." She smirked, clearly hiding something.

Ethan stepped in front of Lizzy, ignoring his racing pulse. "You're hiding something."

Lizzy's laughter warmed his heart. It was genuine, without a hint of holding back. He liked this open side of her.

"Okay. I may not be serving gingerbread people, but I am turning my shop into a gingerbread house. We should be able to start hanging decorations tomorrow." Lizzy's cheeks were red from the cold. "I know we're playing nice for the public, but I still plan on completely destroying you and every other shop in the decorating contest."

Ethan spun her around so he could hug her from behind, resting his cheek against her head. He bent his head so he could whisper in her ear. "You don't have a chance of beating me. The scooter shop, however? It's going down."

Lizzy ducked her head and pulled him forward to the next shop on the street. Ethan kept pace, enjoying the feel of her hand in his.

This shop sold knick knacks from the fifties and sixties. They looked in the window, watching for a few minutes while the owners hung a large plastic bow from the ceiling.

As they watched, he began to dangle small toys from the edges of the bow. They spun lazily back and forth in the window. The fishing line blended in so that it looked like each toy was flying.

"That's pretty creative," Ethan said. He knew the competition would be stiff, but he had hoped at least some of the owners would only do the bare minimum.

"We'll see. I'll have to keep an eye on this shop."

The next shop on the street was Ethan's. His display window was a mess, with tall boards leaning against the sides. The wood had been painted, but only Ethan knew what the designs would be. He had purposefully turned the wood so no one could see the fronts.

"Now this store has an especially unique decorating style." Lizzy pulled him forward. "I personally am getting a crossover vibe between unpacking the tree and cleaning out the garage. It's looking at Christmas before everything is put into place."

Ethan tried to tickle her through her coat. The fabric was thick enough, there was no way he was making a difference, but Lizzy shrieked and ran a few steps away. She planted her hands on her hips, a smile dancing across her lips as Ethan caught her in his grasp.

Pulling her into his arms felt natural. Ethan stared into her eyes, gauging the moment. As Lizzy held his gaze, his eyes flickered to her lips. They were opened slightly, the invitation clear.

Ethan's heart began to race. This outing was pretend. The purpose was to let each of the shop owners visibly see them together. He could kiss Lizzy in front of his shop, but that was the one place he knew no photographer would be hiding.

He pressed a kiss to her forehead. "Wrong shop," he muttered. It took a lot of will power to pull Lizzy forward to Irma Mae's window.

She was still supposed to be keeping weight off her hip, but the doctor had given Irma Mae a wheelchair to help her get around. His orders had been strict. She was to stay off her feet while she recovered. He must not have said anything about leaving the house, though, because she was sitting inside her shop.

"She's back," Lizzy exclaimed.

Ethan looked through the space between the Christmas quilts that were displayed in the window, studying Irma Mae's face while she sat behind the counter. "Do you want to go say hi?"

Lizzy's face lit up. "Yes, please. I've missed seeing her around."

"Me, too." Ethan held open the door for Lizzy, waiting to grab her hand again when they both stepped through. It was hard to believe that someone from Irma Mae's shop would try to sabotage them, but they couldn't rule anyone out.

If they were doing their job right, the saboteur would see them together, and hopefully post another picture. They just needed to figure out which shop it was coming from. Each of their employees had been assigned a different store to watch.

Lizzy pulled off her gloves. Ethan followed her lead, removing his own gloves. This time, when she slid her hand in his, heat blasted from his palm through his entire body. He wanted more, but they had a job to do. Dealing with his feelings would have to wait.

CHAPTER 15

❄

*I*rma Mae's face lit up when Lizzy pulled Ethan towards her. "My favorite rescuers!" She wrapped them in a hug, squishing Lizzy against her side. Lizzy didn't mind. She needed a little distance from Ethan and the whirlwind of feelings coursing through her body.

The plan had been to walk down Ethan's side of the street, letting all the shop owners see them together. If someone was trying to sabotage them, they would have plenty of time to snap a photo or two of the happy couple. Her heart, however, was making it difficult to remember the pretend part of the plan.

Maria, Robert, Kitty and Chad were each in a different shop, posing as customers. The plan was for no one to make eye contact, so Lizzy was surprised when Kitty approached them in Irma Mae's shop.

"Hey guys. It's good to see you here." Kitty's voice sounded strained. "Can you help me with something?"

She pulled them over to a small display of thread, raising her voice. "I can't decide if I should use red or green thread for my latest project." Kitty lowered her voice. "There's a woman towards the front of the store who has been taking pictures of you since you came in."

"I like the way the red pops against the white fabric." Thankfully Ethan was keeping a level head because Lizzy's mind was spinning.

"I agree. It will bring out the Christmas cheer." Lizzy tried to add to the conversation, but she was more interested in identifying their mysterious photographer.

"Thanks, guys." Kitty said, loud enough for the woman to hear. She lowered her voice again. "I'll keep an eye out to see what she does."

Lizzy let Ethan pull her over to one of the quilt kits. He bent over to grab the package, lifting it up to shield his face while he spoke. "Ready to sell it to our adoring fan?"

The trembles in Lizzy's hands had nothing to do with the fact that their potential saboteur was standing fifteen feet away. They had discussed what they would do if they caught anyone spying on them, but Lizzy hadn't actually believed they would.

"You have my permission to kiss me," she whispered.

"What about this one?" Ethan asked, holding out the kit. "Do you think that would be a good gift?"

"My mom would love it." It was difficult to hold a regular conversation when Lizzy knew that at any minute, she'd be locking lips with the man she had kissed once before. That time had been a strained situation, but not so strained that she couldn't appreciate how much she had enjoyed the moment. She had dreamed about kissing him almost every day since.

The anticipation was killing her. She threw her hands around Ethan's neck. "You always find the best things."

It was time. Ethan lowered his face and Lizzy slid a hand to his shoulder. His voice was gruff when he grazed his lips against hers. "You sure about this?"

"Absolutely." Lizzy pressed her lips against his, hungry for his touch. She was expecting to enjoy the kiss, but she wasn't prepared for the fireworks that surged through her body.

Time slowed as the kiss became all that Lizzy could think of. She wanted to pull her body closer to his, but he began to pull away. She was disappointed when he broke their embrace a few seconds later, until she remembered where they were standing. Making out with Ethan was something Lizzy was interested in doing, but not in the middle of Irma Mae's quilt shop with an audience watching.

She glanced towards Kitty, who gave a slight nod of her head. It was time to get out of the shop and see if any pictures got posted.

Lizzy cleared her throat. "I think we've found a winner, but I want to check out a few more shops before I make my final decision. My mom is so hard to shop for."

"You're right. We should check out all our options."

Ethan waved goodbye to Irma Mae while Lizzy looked at the other customers, including the woman who had been taking pictures of them. She seemed familiar, but Lizzy couldn't put a finger on why.

She waited until they were outside the store before turning to bury her face in Ethan's chest. His arms wrapped around her, holding her close.

"I can't believe you were right." Ethan stroked her hair. "I mean, I thought you were, but finding someone who is actually taking pictures is creepy."

Lizzy tilted her head back to look at him. "I agree. I'm not sure what we're supposed to do now." She shivered, and Ethan ran his hands up and down her arms, trying to warm her up.

"I think we should finish our shopping. For all we know, the woman is going to come out that door any second and keep following us."

"So we keep up the ruse?"

"Exactly." Ethan held out his hand. "Besides, you probably need to see the rest of the windows for the competition. So you know who you'll be beating out for second place."

She shoved out of his arms with a laugh. "You wish, baker boy."

Ethan's eyes shot up. "Baker boy? Is that supposed to be an insult?"

"Not at all. I like a man who knows his way around the kitchen." Lizzy reached for his arm, resting her hand in the crook of his elbow. "Besides, that is what you are."

He studied her face, the moment stretching on until she broke their eye contact with a laugh. If they didn't start moving, the photographer was going to be suspicious.

The display in the tackle shop next to Irma Mae's caused them to stop, their mouths hanging open. The shop was never busy. Lizzy had seen so few people walking in and out of the doors, she almost forgot it existed.

It might be forgotten most of the week, but the owners weren't playing around when it came to the decorating contest. A small boat filled the window from side to side, decked out with lights and ball ornaments that hung off the edge. Sitting inside the boat were two elves, holding on to paddles painted like candy canes.

The centerpiece of the window was jaw dropping, but the decorations didn't stop there. Santa sat in the back of the boat, holding a fishing rod. The lower third of the window held small fish which swam back and forth, each wearing a different style of Santa hat.

Ethan was the first to speak. "I guess we have a little competition."

Lizzy wanted to press her nose to the pane of glass. The designer was a master of illusions, hiding the mechanics of the scene so that all the casual passerby saw was Santa and his elves rowing slowly across the pond with fish swimming beneath them.

Somewhere in the display there had to be hidden strings, springs, or strong magnets. Otherwise, the movement didn't make sense. As Lizzy watched, she began to see the wires, carefully disguised throughout the display.

For the first time since hearing about the contest, Lizzy worried that she might not have what it took to win.

She became aware of Ethan, pressed against her side while he studied the display. It felt comfortable having him beside her, like he would protect her from anything. She felt a twinge of remorse for wasting so much time being rude when they could have been building a friendship.

As Lizzy stepped back from the window, she leaned into Ethan's arms. "Any sighting of our shadow?" She spoke softly just in case the woman was there.

In response, Ethan turned her so she was facing him. "She just came out of the store. Laugh like I said something hilarious."

Lizzy tilted her head back with a laugh which quickly turned to a gasp of delight when Ethan trailed kisses up her neck to her mouth. For a few moments, all she could think about was wanting more. All too soon, he broke the kiss.

It was easy to get caught up in the bubble with Ethan. They were putting on a show for a nosy busy body, but his kisses felt a little too real.

Her heart was racing out of her chest when he pressed his forehead to hers. His ragged breathing told her that maybe he wasn't as casual as he seemed to be.

"She's leaving now. I guess we gave her what she wanted." Ethan stepped back, breaking their romantic bubble. He dropped her hand and stuffed his hands back in his pockets. "We did good."

"Mmm hmm." Lizzy didn't trust herself to speak. Ethan was doing exactly what they had planned, following their carefully scripted movements perfectly. She was the one reading too much into every touch.

"Are you okay?" Ethan's eyes looked concerned. "What did I do wrong?"

It was tempting to walk away from Ethan. They had enjoyed a fun moment of window shopping, even if their time together had been short. Lizzy didn't owe Ethan any explanation, but she didn't want to lie to him anymore.

"The only thing you did wrong was act like a perfect gentleman again. We got what we wanted, and now we can hopefully figure out who is behind the sabotage." She wasn't saying what she wanted to say.

He misunderstood. "Don't worry. We'll catch them."

Lizzy shook her head. "It's not that. I mean, yes, I hope we catch them, but that's not what is on my mind."

Ethan raised an eyebrow. "What's wrong, then?"

The time for cowardice was long gone. Lizzy squared her shoulders. "The problem is that even though this was all a trap to catch our peeping Tom, I liked it a little too much. I'm going to be honest. I like kissing you a lot more than I should." She took a deep breath. "I know we're supposed to be at odds, with our competing shops, but what if we weren't?"

Ethan's face was impossible to read. He fiddled with the zipper on his coat. "Are you saying you want to date me?"

Lizzy didn't stop to analyze her words. "I do. I mean, if

things were different, you'd be the cute guy who asked me out in the coffee shop. We wouldn't have competing stores or months of me shutting you out. We'd be real friends. Maybe even a real couple."

The words were spewing out of her mouth, but in that moment, Lizzy didn't care. She had already embarrassed herself so many times in front of Ethan, it felt normal. She bit the side of her cheek and turned away.

Ethan pressed his hand to her shoulder. When she looked in his direction, his eyes were smoldering. He opened his mouth as if to speak, but then he shook his head slightly.

Lizzy closed her eyes. This was the part where he walked away. She gasped when he pressed his lips to hers, light and gentle. He pulled back slightly but this time Lizzy wasn't having it. If this was the last kiss she was going to have with Ethan, she was going to make it a good one.

She cupped a hand around his neck, pulling his face close. This time, when their lips met, there was no hesitation. Lizzy tried to memorize the feel of his mouth pressing against hers. His lips were cold, but they quickly warmed up.

The seconds ticked by, but instead of breaking away, Ethan slid his hands to her waist and pulled her closer. A part of Lizzy's brain tried to remind her that she was standing in the middle of a very public sidewalk, locking lips with a man, but she didn't care. Being a shop owner didn't mean that she had to give up her personal life.

Lizzy pressed her hand to Ethan's chest, wishing she could feel his heart beneath the layers of his coat. Time lost all meaning as she focused on every detail about Ethan, from the smell of his skin to the softness of his mouth against hers. She ran a hand down his cheek, his five o' clock shadow rough beneath her fingers.

Far too soon, Ethan pulled away, but he didn't let go of her waist. "In case you missed it, I kind of enjoy kissing you, too."

"So, what does this mean?" Lizzy tried to calm her racing pulse, but looking into Ethan's eyes was making that difficult to do.

"I think that it means that maybe I should take you out on a real date. Like people do who aren't trying to compete with each other's shops."

"Hmm." The thought was incredibly tempting. "I think that's a great idea."

Ethan brushed her hair back. "So, what does the rest of your week look like?"

"I don't know. I'm kind of busy trying to win a decorating contest." Lizzy winked. "Although, from what I see of the competition, it's going to be a piece of cake."

Ethan lifted her chin, leaning his face down so he was inches from her mouth. "Bring it."

He smirked and straightened up, steering them back towards his shop where the employees were waiting to give their reports.

* * *

WAITING for the saboteur to post pictures was agony. Kitty had snapped a photo of the stalker when they were inside the quilt shop. Lizzy couldn't shake the nagging feeling that it was someone she had crossed paths with before. The problem was that she couldn't remember who it was or why the lady would be holding a grudge.

There was no sense in agonizing over it. Judging for the decorating contest was starting in a few days and Lizzy's vision was finally coming to life. She kept an eye on the other stores to track their progress. A few of them had put up incredible displays but she knew she was just as competitive.

Lizzy was adjusting the candy in her display window when she glanced at Ethan's shop. She told herself that it was so she could keep up with the competition, but every time she looked that way, her heart fluttered. She was hoping to catch a glimpse of Ethan.

After the meeting with their employees, he had kissed her until she was breathless. She drove home that night with her head floating in the clouds. That had been two days ago, and she hadn't seen him since. The paranoid side of her brain created all sorts of scenarios, including the idea that he was trying to use his charm to throw her off her game.

She was reaching for another wrapped candy when she finally spotted Ethan, his brow furrowed in concentration while he tinkered with his display. He had gone all out, creating a winter ski resort in his window. Wood panels locked together to form a ski lodge that Ethan set on a tall mountain, tucked to one side of the display.

Penguins and polar bears skied down the slope, heading for a miniature version of Ethan's Crumbs at the bottom. There was a line of animals waiting to get in, including some impatient reindeer. A few happy customers sat at tables scattered to the side of the shop, holding cookies in their paws.

The display was certainly eye catching, but as far as Lizzy could see, it didn't extend into the shop. Hers did, which would hopefully give her an edge.

Lizzy fastened a fake candy cane to the side of the wall. When she glanced up again, Ethan was gone. She tamped down the disappointment that surged through her. There would be time to daydream about Ethan when she was off work.

It was time to start fine tuning all the details of the decorations. Her window was the outside of a gingerbread house with candy sides and frosted shingles. Most of the display framed the large window that gave the customer a chance to look inside Lizzy's shop.

The entire inside of the shop was transforming into a gingerbread house, with gigantic, wrapped candies hanging on every wall. The countertops were draped with wavy sheets that hung down like icing. Each table had been topped with a bright tablecloth; the tops dotted with speckles to look like gumdrops.

Lizzy's goal was to make the entire inside of the store

so tempting, people would come in and buy a cookie or two before continuing on their way.

She headed to the back room to pull out more decorations. The weeks of painting paper plates and wrapping them in cellophane had paid off. Each decoration looked like something you'd buy in a store, but the entire display cost very little money.

Lizzy held up two different sizes of candy, choosing to go with the smaller design. She brought an armful to the front and hung them from the ceiling. The red and green swirls would add a pop of color to the brown gingerbread, but she didn't want them to block the magical view inside.

She headed outside to look at the display from the street, shivering when the cold air blew through her sweater. Lizzy was studying the candies when a coat was draped over her shoulders.

"It's far too cold to be outside." Ethan slid his arms around her waist. "What are you doing out here?"

Lizzy leaned back against Ethan's chest, her breath hitching in her throat. She could sink into his embrace for hours, letting work go to the side, but they both had jobs to do. If she couldn't have hours, she could enjoy the few minutes they had.

The coat wrapped around her shoulders clearly belonged to Ethan. "There's a problem here. Now you're the one outside without a coat." Lizzy shrugged it off her shoulders and handed it back. "I know how to fix this."

She waited for Ethan to put the coat back on, ignoring his

protests. Once he was dressed, she stepped into his arms and leaned her cheek against his chest, wrapping her arms around his back so the jacket was around both of them. Ethan grabbed the edges of the coat and pulled them closed so Lizzy was nestled inside the folds of fabric, next to his heart.

This time, without layers of a heavy coat in the way, Lizzy closed her eyes and concentrated until she could hear Ethan's heartbeat. It was racing, a match to her own rapid pulse.

Ethan pressed a kiss to the top of her head. "Two days is way too long to go without seeing you."

"I agree." She wanted to sink into his embrace and let the worries of the world pass them by.

He kissed her again, this time on the forehead. "So, what were you doing out here without proper warmth?"

Lizzy took a deep breath, smelling the molasses that clung to his clothes. "I'm trying to decide if I like the hanging candies or not. They don't seem quite right."

Ethan kissed one cheek, and then the other. "I like them. Have you tried it with fewer of them? It won't feel so crowded."

He was right. Removing half the candies would make it less cluttered so the eye would be drawn inside.

"I'll see how it looks. Now, I know you didn't come across the street to help me win the decorating contest. What's up?"

Ethan tilted her head up so he could brush a kiss across her lips. "First, I missed kissing you."

Tingles raced through Lizzy's body, filling it with warmth even though the air outside was freezing.

"And second?" Lizzy was pretty sure she knew the answer.

Ethan rubbed her back. "She finally posted a picture."

CHAPTER 16

❄

*E*than waited for Lizzy's cry of dismay to come. Instead, she ran a hand up and down his back.

"Is it bad?" Her voice was a little shaky, but Ethan couldn't tell if it was from the cold or the news.

"Let's go inside so we can talk. My shop or yours?" He wasn't going to pull out the picture while they were freezing on the sidewalk.

"Mine is closer." Lizzy pulled out of Ethan's warm embrace and ran to her store.

When Ethan entered the store, his jaw dropped. Almost overnight, it had transformed into a life-sized gingerbread house. The attention to detail was incredible. "Please tell me you've decided to sell gingerbread cookies. How can you not?"

Lizzy grinned. "No prying for company secrets." She pulled him into the office, closing the door behind him. "Don't tell anyone, but yes. I'm going to be featuring gingerbread people all month. I'm not sure how popular of a flavor it is, but I hope they'll sell well."

The woman standing in front of him was incredible. Ethan wasn't sure what the future held for their shops, but he hoped whatever happened, they'd be able to navigate it as more than friends.

He sat in the chair Lizzy pointed to and pulled out his phone. "She posted about ten minutes ago. Chad found it when he was on break. This time, the woman didn't hold back the punches."

Lizzy reached for the phone, her mouth pressing into a thin line while she read.

I have lived in this town all my life. It is a city that has been founded on family values, integrity, and hard work. I am amazed that the mayor continues to look the other way when two businesses are openly trying to flaunt their dishonesty in our faces.

Ethan Crandall and Lizzy Thompson are clearly dating. They lied about their relationship, which makes me wonder what else they are lying about. Real estate on historic Main Street is limited to small, single owner shops. Not corporations. Clearly Crandall and Thompson found a way to get around that restriction. They lied and cheated their way into acquiring two properties to gain more business for their cookie empire. They are working together to put the other shops on the street out of business.

I request that Mayor Bliss and the town council force the cookie shop owners to consolidate into one space, making way for a different kind of shop. I hope the town will get behind this request. Shopping at either place shows your support of dishonest practices. Let's keep Main Street diverse.

There was a heavy silence in the room when she met Ethan's eyes. "You were right about her not holding back. That is one of the rudest posts I've seen in a long time."

Ethan nodded. "I agree. I'm not sure what we did to offend her, but she clearly has a grudge. Calling us liars and cheats is a little extreme."

"How did she put it?" Lizzy scrolled down the post. "Oh yeah. We're secretly working together to put other shops on the street out of business."

Ethan rubbed his hands together. "I'm not sure how she got ahold of my business plan. Step one. Open a shop. Step two. In all my spare time, work with my competitor to take out everyone else." He pressed his hand to the table. "It doesn't make any sense. How on earth would putting anyone out of business help us? I personally love it when customers come in carrying bags from Irma Mae's shop. She brought the business to her shop, but I can be the final stop on their trip."

"Exactly." Lizzy pulled her light brown hair out of the bun, shaking it out before she twisted it back up on her head. A few strands hung down, framing her face. "The whole point of a community is that everyone works together. I didn't see anyone complaining when we helped Irma Mae. Or the motorists."

The bouncing of Ethan's knee was shaking his entire body. It was a nervous habit that he couldn't stop when he was agitated. "The post is ridiculous, but you know people in this town are. If they believe, even for a minute, that we are plotting to take down Main Street, they are going to revolt. We have to write a rebuttal."

"How do you feel about making a video together?" Lizzy's eyes were bright with excitement. "I mean, this time, her latest picture may actually help us dispel any rumors."

Ethan didn't want to admit that he had saved the picture from the post to his phone. He was holding Lizzy in the picture, gazing at her with a look of pure adoration while they stood outside the tackle shop. This was taken right after she had kissed him. From any outsider's perspective, Ethan and Lizzy were clearly falling in love.

"I like it. What do we say?"

Lizzy bit the side of her cheek. "I guess for starters we should address the rumor that we're trying to put the other shops out of business."

"What about our relationship?" Ethan was curious what Lizzy would say.

She teased the side of her lip. "How about we try filming and see what comes out?"

Ethan nodded. "That sounds good. I was thinking we could film it from one of the tables in your shop. They look great."

"Thanks." Lizzy pushed back her chair. "Wait here. I'll see if the coast is clear." She ducked out the door, and Ethan was left in the office.

He took the time to study each detail of the room, from the way she shoved papers into a cluttered pile on her desk to the framed pictures she had on her walls. There were a couple of family photos. It was easy to see where Lizzy had gotten her smile from.

Lizzy came back a few minutes later. "The coast is clear. Maria said she'd film for us.

Ethan's hands began to shake. He wasn't comfortable in front of a camera.

Before he could overthink things, Lizzy was cupping her hands behind his neck. "Don't worry. I've got you." She kissed his lips softly like he was someone that could break.

Walking out of the office to film the rebuttal felt like an impossible task, but Ethan tried to remember what he was doing there. He and Lizzy had a job to do, and he wasn't going to fail her.

He reached for her hand. "I'm ready."

Two minutes later, Ethan was ready to take his words back. His mouth went dry when Maria held up the phone to record them. "I have no idea what I'm going to say."

"Just follow my lead. We'll start with introductions and see how it goes." Lizzy rubbed his arm. "You'll do great."

"If you say so." Ethan gulped, sinking into the chair.

"Ready?" Maria asked.

Lizzy reached for Ethan's hand under the table, giving it a reassuring squeeze. She nodded at Maria and the camera turned on.

"Hi friends. I'm Lizzy Thompson, owner of Cookies by Liz. And this is . . .". She trailed off, waiting for Ethan.

He grinned sheepishly at the camera. "Sorry, guys. I'm

not used to this sort of thing. I'm Ethan Crandall, owner of the Ethan's Crumbs cookie shop."

Lizzy's hand was steadying his nerves. She gave it a little squeeze before continuing to speak. "There has been a lot of buzz in the community since you discovered there were going to be two cookie shops on the same block. The only people more surprised than you were us, the two owners who both thought we had unique shops."

She was doing a great job. Ethan watched Lizzy's face light up as she spoke. She was mesmerizing. She winked at Ethan. "I didn't exactly handle the news well, did I?"

Ethan realized he was supposed to answer. He ran his free hand through his hair, refusing to let go of Lizzy's hand. "Let's just say we had a couple of disagreements while trying to get our shops off the ground." Ethan laughed. "Okay. That's putting it too mildly. I thought Lizzy couldn't stand me."

"And I thought he was purposely trying to steal my dreams." Lizzy bumped his shoulder with hers.

Ethan couldn't help but smile. "Eventually we realized that we have far more in common than we thought."

Lizzy stroked the back of his hand. Her face fell. "The problem is that someone in the community is trying to ruin our reputations. We thought we'd make this little video to clear some things up."

"For starters," Ethan said, "the idea that we're trying to put anyone out of business is absurd. We love being part of a community. Every shop owner we've met has become a friend."

"We aren't one big company trying to con you out of your money by buying up all the stores on Main Street." Lizzy shook her head. "We're two very independent store owners who happen to love the best dessert in the world."

She looked at Ethan, raising her eyebrows.

He got the signal. "As for the other rumors, I personally can't imagine why it would matter if Lizzy and I were dating or not. Our personal life has nothing to do with the way we sell our cookies."

He looked straight into the camera. "Since everyone seems so interested, I'll clear up a couple of things. No, we haven't been secretly dating for months. Yes, we've gotten a lot closer over the past few weeks."

It was Lizzy's turn to speak before Ethan started professing his utter infatuation with her.

She turned to study Ethan's face, and Ethan was grateful that the camera couldn't pick up the electricity flowing through his body.

"To put it bluntly, I'm crazy about the guy." Lizzy gave Ethan a smile before turning her attention back to the phone. "I don't know what the future holds for us, but we'd ask the community to be kind. It's hard enough trying to run a shop without rumors flying around."

"Hopefully that helps to clear some things up." Ethan's nerves were beginning to calm. "If you have any questions, be sure to ask them in the comments section. We really don't have anything to hide."

He turned his attention to Lizzy, hoping she'd bring it home.

"Thanks for hearing our side of things. Merry Christmas!"

Maria turned off the camera and Ethan leaned back, staring at the ceiling. His heart was pounding out of his chest like he had just run a marathon. "That was stressful."

"You did great." Lizzy kissed his cheek. "I'll post it now and then we'll see what happens."

* * *

HEADING BACK to his shop was difficult. Ethan had enjoyed filming the video with Lizzy far more than he expected. He was ready to ask her out on an official date.

An hour before the shops closed, Ethan realized that he was running out of time. He wanted to walk back over to her shop and ask in person, but the steady stream of customers never let up. He settled for a text message, checking his phone every two seconds until she answered with a yes.

The last half hour before closing went slower than the entire rest of the day. Ethan couldn't wait to see Lizzy. They were going to go to dinner together, on a real date like typical couples did.

His nerves didn't kick in until he was standing in front of her store, wishing he had thought to get flowers.

Lizzy was sweeping the floor when he knocked on the door. Her face lit up when she unlocked it to let him in.

"Do you need any help?" Ethan was surprised to see that the employees were gone.

She shook her head as she flicked the last bits of dirt into the dustpan and emptied it over the trash can. "That was the last of it. I'm ready to go."

Ethan reached for Lizzy's hand. "Are you craving anything in particular, or would you like me to surprise you."

"Surprise, please."

At the edge of town were two burger shops which stood on opposite corners. The town debate for years had been which shop served the best fries. They were Ethan's inspiration whenever he started to think that there wasn't room for two shops who served similar foods.

Gary's had a special fry sauce that mixed barbeque sauce with mayonnaise. People bought it by the bottle full because it was just that good. The competitor, Nate's, served smothered fries that were a heart attack waiting to happen. They were loaded with nacho cheese sauce, bacon, and green onions and topped with a dollop of sour cream and diced tomatoes.

Ethan pulled into the first parking space he saw.

"Nate's?" Lizzy asked. "I haven't been here in ages. Last I heard, they had a new menu."

"I thought we could try food from both. Let's order one meal from Nate's and one from Gary's. We can do a taste test to see who we like best."

A chilly blast of wind met their faces when they climbed out of the car. "It does get warmer here eventually, right?" Ethan was tired of the snow.

"Yes." Lizzy looped her arm through his and he clamped

his hand down over it, holding tight so she wouldn't slip in the snow that was beginning to fall. They put their order in and stood near a heater while they waited for their number to be called.

"Did you read any of the comments yet?" Ethan asked.

Lizzy shook her head. "I didn't want to have to deal with it at work."

"Neither did I. I guess we can check them when we get back to my house."

"We're going to your house?" Lizzy bumped him with her arm. "I can't wait to see where you live. Do I get to meet Cindy?"

Ethan grinned. "I've told her a lot about you."

"I hope she isn't too harsh of a judge. I wouldn't want her to be disappointed."

"She does judge people based on their cuddling levels." Ethan's eyes crinkled when he studied her face. "Then again, based on my experience, you'll do just fine." He pressed a kiss to her cheek.

Lizzy was laughing when their number was called.

The order at Gary's went even faster. Ethan blasted the heat on the way home in an attempt to keep them warm.

Lizzy's face lit up when they walked into the apartment. She dropped to her knees when Cindy came trotting out of the bedroom. "Aren't you just the cutest thing ever?"

Ethan slid the bags onto the kitchen table and watched as Lizzy rubbed Cindy's ears. The beagle lay on the ground, her paws in the air, and Ethan smiled. He knew Cindy would be a fan.

After a moment, Lizzy straightened up. "She's adorable."

"I think she likes you." Ethan headed to the kitchen to grab plates and knives while Lizzy pulled out the food.

It took just a second to cut the burgers in half and slide them onto each plate. Ethan pushed the container of fries over to Lizzy, not bothering to divide them out. He watched with anticipation when she dipped a fry into Gary's secret sauce. She popped it in her mouth, chewing slowly.

"What do you think?"

Lizzy opened her eyes slowly. "That was delicious. In fact, I think I may need to try another one or two, or twenty, to make sure I am making an accurate diagnosis."

Ethan laughed, reaching for his own fry to dip. He had eaten at both places before, but never done a side-by-side comparison.

"They really are good. I used to come here after a frustrating day at the shop."

"So, every day?" Lizzy was teasing, but her words hit the mark.

"In the beginning, it felt like it. Did you have any idea how hard all this would be?"

Lizzy dipped a fry and waved it back and forth while she gestured with her hands. "No. I mean, I knew opening a business would be hard work, but this has been such a rollercoaster of emotions. Most days I go home unsure if I want to laugh or cry."

"Exactly." Even though Lizzy was technically his

competitor, it felt good to have someone to talk to. "I love meeting the customers and hearing their stories about what they are buying the cookies for, but the rest is exhausting."

Lizzy nodded while she chewed.

Ethan opened the box of Nate's loaded fries and slid it to the middle of the table between them, handing Lizzy a fork. "We can't have a fair taste test if we let Nate's fries get cold."

The smell of bacon filled the air. Ethan's mouth was already watering when he stabbed a fry, making sure to get a little bit of everything in one bite. Lizzy copied him, raising her fork at the same time.

"May the best fry win." She popped her bite in her mouth, once again taking time to appreciate the flavors. The look of concentration on her face was adorable. When she opened her eyes, Ethan could see her answer.

"Nate's takes the competition, hands down." Lizzy stabbed another fry with cheese dripping down the side. "Which one do you like best?"

Ethan laughed. "I'm actually a Gary's fan, but I will happily eat either of them." He pushed the tray closer to Lizzy. "Enjoy."

Her face lit up. "I can see why you'd go there after hard days. Speaking of which, do we dare to check the reactions to our post, yet?"

"We already have comfort food if the comments are awful." Ethan pulled out his phone. "I'm ready. Are you?"

"Let's do it."

Ethan pulled up the post, his stomach tying in knots. He glanced at the number of comments and then did a double take. "We have over five hundred comments."

Lizzy dropped her fork and slid her chair to his side. "That's impossible."

No matter how fast Ethan scrolled, he couldn't seem to reach the end of them. He met Lizzy's eyes. "What did we do?"

She wrinkled her nose. "I think we stirred the hornet's nest."

CHAPTER 17

❋

*R*eading the comments felt like sitting on a speeding train that was careening wildly back and forth through the mountains. There would be a section praising Lizzy and Ethan, but then, a few comments later, someone would launch into how angry they were, and a negative chain of responses would follow.

Lizzy was silent while she read, glancing up occasionally to gauge Ethan's reactions. His face, like her emotions, flickered back and forth from a stern, furrowed brow to a smirk dancing on his lips.

He was somber when he finally looked up. "Well. That wasn't what I was expecting."

That was the understatement of the year. Lizzy had prepared herself for some resistance to their video, but the responses from the community blew her away.

"Me either."

Ethan's posture hadn't relaxed since they started reading. Lizzy wanted to reach out and smooth down his tense shoulders. The thought of reaching out sent tingles of longing through her body. If they were further along in their budding relationship, they could cuddle on the couch, comforting one another.

As it stood, Lizzy was limited to reaching past the fast-food wrappers to rest her hand on Ethan's. She held his hand until he met her eyes.

"I don't know what we're supposed to do." Ethan usually sounded upbeat, but there was a layer of sadness in his voice when he spoke. "How do we fight rumors?"

"We don't." It was a simple answer, really. If the video of Lizzy and Ethan hadn't been enough to convince the public they were sincere, then nothing would probably work.

Ethan abruptly pushed away from the table, collecting their garbage. Lizzy stood to help but he told her to sit. "I've got it," he said.

Her heart was pounding when he reached out a few minutes later, pulling her to her feet.

"The way I see it, we can sit here, reading comments from internet trolls, or we can head out to do something fun. I vote for fun."

A wave of peace washed over Lizzy. Ethan was right. It didn't matter what the world thought. She was wasting their time together by stressing over what other people were saying and doing.

"You surprised me with our dinner choices. It's my turn to surprise you."

Ethan flashed her a smile, his eyes lighting up. "I'm all yours. Where to?"

* * *

SNOWFLAKES DRIFTED LAZILY through the sky, floating down to rest on her face, which helped to distract Lizzy's mind from the fact that she was standing in the middle of the Victor Ash Gardens, hand in hand with Ethan. They were currently cuddled up next to a large fire pit, sharing the space with two other couples and a family with three younger children.

One of the hidden gems of the city was the Ash Gardens. The local family who owned the property started the garden as a memorial to their son who lost his fight with childhood cancer years before. Every year they added a new set of lights or an attraction to visit. Over the years it had grown from a one-day event in the back-yard to a sprawling event that covered all twenty-five acres of their land and lasted the entire month of December.

Ethan dropped her hand and stepped behind her, wrapping his arms around her waist before he rested his chin on her head. "This is magical," he murmured.

"I've been coming every year since it opened. I even kept coming once my parents moved. It's part of my holiday traditions now."

"Did you ever meet the family?"

Lizzy shook her head, aware of the pressure of Ethan's

chin. "Not back then, but I recognize them now if I see them around town."

Warm tendrils of smoke blew towards Lizzy and Ethan, the flames crackling around heavy logs. There was a sense of quiet comradery that filled the space, even though they were sharing it with other people. Lizzy appreciated how comfortable she felt standing in silence with Ethan. She didn't feel the need for awkward conversation.

She slid her hands along Ethan's arms, stroking them back and forth. It was difficult to remember how angry she had been when they first met. He felt like a close friend now; someone she could confide in.

The family across from them opened a bag, offering marshmallows around the group. The gardens provided skewers for people to roast their own food. Some years, the smell of hot dogs would waft through the air. Lizzy had never been tempted to bring any food of her own.

Ethan took the bag of marshmallows, pulling out a small handful. He reached for a skewer and stabbed three marshmallows onto the end before handing it over.

Lizzy missed the warmth of Ethan behind her, but she took the skewer with a smile. "Want to see who can make the best toasted marshmallow?"

Ethan loaded three marshmallows onto his skewer before passing the bag to his neighbor. "You're on."

His brow furrowed with concentration. Lizzy laughed and kissed him on the cheek. "Good luck."

She turned her focus to the skewer, slowly turning it in the heat so each marshmallow would warm up at the same time. They were getting a golden tint when Ethan yelped beside her. His top marshmallow was on fire, flames licking towards the other two marshmallows.

Watching Ethan blow out his marshmallows distracted Lizzy just long enough for her hand to slip, catching her own marshmallows on fire. She held them up with a groan.

Ethan blew her torched marshmallows out as well, shaking his head back and forth with a grin. He leaned close, his voice tickling her ear. "Good thing no one knows we bake for a living, right?"

Lizzy propped the skewer on the edge of the fire pit so she could pull off her gloves. Charred or not, Lizzy was prepared to eat her work. She pulled off the first marshmallow which had gotten the brunt of the fire, popping it into her mouth.

Ethan raised an eyebrow at her.

"It's delicious," she said. "Maybe I'll add a toasted s'mores cookie to my menu."

"You mean a charred s'mores flavor?" Ethan removed his own gloves and pulled the marshmallow off, licking his fingers after he ate.

He turned to look at Lizzy and her heart skipped a beat. His eyes reflected the flickering flame and Lizzy knew she would be happy staring into those eyes all night. He leaned down to brush a soft kiss across her lips that tasted sugary sweet. The temptation to lean in for more was strong, but Lizzy remembered the company they were keeping. The family who shared the marshmallows certainly didn't need to be next to an uncomfortable make out session.

She settled for the next best thing, grabbing Ethan's hand before either of them could pull the gloves back on. The warmth of his hand blasted through her body when she locked her fingers with his.

In response, Ethan lifted her hand to his lips, kissing each finger individually.

Whatever the future held for them, Lizzy knew that she would cherish this night. "Are you ready to go see the lights?"

Ethan glanced down, giving her hand a gentle squeeze. "Does that mean that I am going to have to let go of your hand? Because I'm not sure I like that option."

"It depends. Do you want us to have frostbite by the end of the night?" The cold air was already making Lizzy's fingers feel like small popsicles.

"Good point." Ethan rubbed the back of her hand with his thumb, the trails of heat warming her more thoroughly than a glove ever could.

He let go, and it took all of Lizzy's willpower not to grab his hand back. She pulled on her glove and reached for his arm. "Let's go see the displays."

Walking through the various light displays felt like walking through a magical wonderland. Lizzy couldn't stop sneaking glances at Ethan's face to watch his reaction to each new display. Her heart skipped a beat every time his eyes lit up.

Her plans had been concrete. There was supposed to be

no dating until her shop was successful. She had barely been open for a month, and clearly not profitable yet, but her heart was determined to break the rules. The giddiness that hit every time she talked to Ethan certainly didn't care about any set schedule.

"What's on your mind?" Ethan's voice cut through her thoughts.

"You are."

Ethan's smile warmed her heart. "I think I'm okay with that. Anything in particular?"

They were approaching a small nativity scene, set back from the path. Lizzy pulled Ethan to a stop so they could look at all the details. The closer they looked; the more flaws Lizzy could see.

A burnt-out section of lights ran across the back of the manger, difficult to see amidst all the bright lights. One of the shepherds was askew, so he was looking off into the distance instead of at the nativity.

"Are we like this display?" Lizzy rubbed her nose where her scarf tickled it. "Everything looks right, but what if we are missing all the little things that are wrong?"

"The display looks great to me." Ethan's brow wrinkled while he studied the figures. "What are you seeing that I'm not?"

"For starters, some of the lights are out."

"Mmm hmm."

"And some of the figures are in the wrong places."

Ethan brushed Lizzy's hair back, making her lose her

train of thought. He hugged her from behind, gently swaying back and forth.

"Do you want to know what I see?" Ethan's breath was warm against her ear.

Lizzy nodded, not trusting herself to speak.

"I see a stable that was put together by someone who clearly isn't a master carpenter. The person who built this stable didn't get every measurement right, but the end result was perfect. They say Jesus was born in humble circumstances. Well, this is about as humble as it gets."

Lizzy followed his finger to look at the star he pointed at. "That star is clearly missing a few bulbs, but it is one of the brightest parts of this display. I'd be able to find this star even if a dozen more lights burnt out."

He lowered his voice to a whisper. "The Savior had a village of people who helped raise him. I see shepherds and wisemen who came from afar to worship a small baby. They believed in something much larger than themselves, and I'd like to think they were patient enough to see his potential unfold."

Ethan rested his chin on her head. "I know our relationship is still new, and we've had a lot of missteps along the way, but I'd like to think that together, we're building something we'll be proud to look at. I don't care if we're missing a few bulbs or if our stable is built with our share of crooked boards. I have the patience to see what unfolds."

The words melted Lizzy's heart. She turned to face him, pressing her cheek against his chilly jacket. A second later, Ethan was wrapping his arms around her.

"You're right." Lizzy kissed Ethan on the cheek. "The little things don't matter."

"Even if they're little pieces of gossip, right?" He was teasing, but Lizzy could hear the concern beneath his light tone.

"Especially if they're bits of gossip. I don't care what our negative stalker has to say. I plan to keep my shop for years to come, and you'd better be planning to keep yours as well."

The glint in Ethan's eye was difficult to miss. "Do you really think I'd let you have all the fun? You need some good competition."

"Game on." Lizzy was laughing when she pulled him through the rest of the gardens. By the time they got to the final display, Lizzy knew more about Ethan than she could have guessed. He was an incredible person who cared for everyone around him. She couldn't believe she had judged him so harshly in the beginning.

They headed to the car, shivering against the cold. The date was coming to a close, but Lizzy didn't want it to be. She rubbed her hands down her arms, waiting for the heater to kick on. There had to be a better way to warm up.

"How do you feel about one more surprise?" Lizzy watched Ethan's face, hoping he felt the same way she did.

"Definitely. I'm not ready for this evening to end." Ethan leaned across the middle console of the car, giving her a small peck on the lips. "Where to, boss?"

Fifteen minutes later they were pulling up to the street in front of a food truck. Lizzy pulled Ethan out of the car, hoping their short stand in the cold air would be worth it. The doughnuts and cocoa served from the food truck were some of her favorite treats.

Lizzy paid more attention to Ethan's face than she did the woman helping them. He toyed with his bottom lip while he tried to decide which doughnuts to order, which reminded her how much she enjoyed kissing those lips.

"I'd recommend our flavor of the month," the woman said. "We fill the center of the doughnuts with mint Oreos."

"And they're delicious." Lizzy had tried every flavor the truck had to offer. She smiled when Ethan tugged her to his side, wrapping an arm around her shoulders.

"What do you recommend?" He looked at her face, putting a lot of trust in the decision.

"Would it be too crazy to get a half-dozen? That way we can try a little bit of each one. You could bring the leftovers to work."

Ethan grinned. "I like the way you think." He ordered one of each flavor, along with two large cups of cocoa. He was lifting his card to pay when he froze.

Lizzy didn't notice the problem at first. She realized something was off when his grip around her shoulders tightened. Lead trickled through her veins as she registered his body language. His lips were pressed together, the teasing smile gone.

"Thank you," he said tersely, pocketing his credit card.

Lizzy let Ethan lead her away, moving them back until they were standing several feet away from the window.

"What's wrong?" She was desperate to wipe the concern off his face.

"Did you see the lady in the truck?" He looked over his shoulder like he was afraid someone was going to catch them talking.

"The woman helping us? I wasn't really paying attention." Worry swirled through her stomach.

"Not her. The one who was helping in the back. I think her name tag said Connie?" Ethan angled his body, so his back was to the truck, shielding Lizzy from the view of the window. "Wasn't she the one taking pictures of us?"

A blast of wind blew past, but the shiver Lizzy felt ran deeper than the cold air. The woman in Irma Mae's shop had looked familiar, but Lizzy hadn't been able to place her until she saw her standing in the truck. Now she knew why she had recognized her. Connie had served her doughnuts several times over the years.

"What are we supposed to do?' Lizzy was willing to leave their doughnuts behind and get out of the situation, but Ethan had paid. She wasn't going to waste his money.

"I'm not sure. I'd like to confront her and ask her why she is so angry at us, but I don't know if that is the right thing to do. She's clearly working right now. It wouldn't be fair to their customers."

"Yeah." Lizzy agreed with his logic. She knew she'd be devastated if someone came to her work and started yelling at her. She slid a few inches to the side so she could see past Ethan's shoulder. The woman was definitely the person who had been taking their pictures. That meant she was most likely the one posting anonymously on the community page.

"Order twenty-seven," the cashier called out. The blackmailer didn't seem to be paying any attention to the customers.

"I'm going to wait by the car," Lizzy said. "If you grab the food, maybe Connie won't notice you. I don't want her to see us together."

Ethan nodded. "I'll see you in a second." He pulled his hat lower, but Lizzy knew the disguise wouldn't work. His face had been splashed across social media. She was shocked the woman hadn't turned around when they had been ordering. Ethan had a deep voice that was distinct.

Moments later, Ethan was sliding into the car, passing over the box of doughnuts. "Now what?" He handed Lizzy her cocoa.

"First, we taste these doughnuts. She may have an agenda, but the doughnuts didn't do anything to hurt us. Then we can figure out what to do."

CHAPTER 18

❄

The box of doughnuts sitting on Ethan's lap felt heavy, a weight that was going to drag him down. Their blackmailer was a woman who served desserts to people, just like he and Lizzy did. How could Connie want to destroy their shops when she most likely shared similar hopes and dreams?

Ethan was pulling the lid open when he noticed the sticker in the bottom corner of the box.

Keep Main Street diverse.

There could be another explanation, but Ethan's stomach plummeted. The community posts had been very vocal about not wanting two cookie shops on the same street. He showed the sticker to Lizzy.

"Were there any other bids on your shop when you bought it?"

Lizzy nodded. "There were a couple. Why?"

"Because I think Connie was trying to buy one of the

spaces on Main Street."

Lizzy's smile fell. "And we both edged her out?"

"Yep. And I think that's why she's so angry." Ethan knew in his gut he was right. "I guess, when you look at it from her perspective, I can see why she'd be sad that she lost the shop space."

The fire in Lizzy's eyes was back. "That doesn't give her any reason to try to hurt us. What is she hoping to do? Drive one of us out of business so she can move from a food truck to an actual shop?"

She reached for the door handle, but Ethan reached for her arm. "What are you planning to do?"

"I'm going to give her a piece of my mind. A few slanderous pictures online are one thing. Openly advertising her agenda to every customer who comes by is something different entirely. You don't treat people like that."

Ethan rubbed his hand up and down her arm, trying to take some of the fire out of Lizzy's glare. "I'm not sure if that would help the situation."

Lizzy pulled away from his touch and he quickly dropped his hand. She wasn't a wild animal that he had to keep caged. She was an independent woman who was allowed to yell at anyone she wanted.

"Can we talk it through before you tear her head off?" Ethan folded his hands in his lap, alarmed at how quickly their date had gone off the rails. He knew Lizzy had a feisty side. He had been on the receiving end of it, and he didn't want to see her upset again.

"Connie is trying to ruin our shops." Lizzy's voice held

layers of anger that Ethan hadn't heard since the day they met.

"I know."

"She can't do that."

"I agree." There was nothing Ethan could do to fix the situation. He felt like no matter what he said, it would be the wrong answer. "What do you want me to do?"

Lizzy looked back and forth between Ethan's face and the woman in the truck. She drummed her fingers against her leg. "Ugh. The rational side of me knows we should probably take these doughnuts back to your place so we can eat our emotions. I really don't want to eat anything she made, though. Even if it is delicious."

"We don't have to eat any, although technically we already paid for them. She wouldn't know the difference." Ethan slid the box of doughnuts to the back seat. "What if we head home? We can regroup there."

He waited for her to answer even though every instinct in his body was telling him to throw the car into drive and get as far away from the food truck as possible. It was so much easier to avoid the potential for a confrontation rather than staying in the danger zone when emotions were high. Still, he respected Lizzy enough to let her work through her feelings.

Headlights pulled up behind Ethan's car. He had gotten a good spot on the street right in front of the doughnut truck that someone else would be happy to take. Lizzy's sigh was audible next to him.

"Let's go home."

That was all the permission Ethan needed. He pulled onto the road, heading towards his house. The lighthearted banter of the evening had vanished, replaced by a heaviness that was difficult to erase. Connie may not have ruined their shops yet, but she had certainly ruined their date.

* * *

FIVE DAYS LATER, Ethan was no closer to finding an answer to the Connie situation than he had been when he and Lizzy had discovered her. The constant war between wanting to treat her with kindness versus retaliation was real. They knew who was spreading lies about the shops. It would be so easy to put Connie and her doughnuts on a social media blast, but that would be stooping to her level. The last thing he or Lizzy needed was a smear campaign.

Instead, he turned his focus to the shop and gearing up for the holiday orders that were starting to come in. The winner of the window decorating contest would be announced at the end of the week, which meant that dozens of customers were coming by daily and peering in the windows before coming in to taste a cookie or two. Many of them placed orders.

As the other shops down Main Street continued to put up their decorations, Ethan knew that the odds of him winning the competition were slim to none. Some of the older shops had pulled out all the stops, their windows rivaling that of shops in New York City.

The one shop that was still in the running was Lizzy's. Somehow, despite a microscopic budget, Lizzy had managed to create a truly magnificent display. Ethan loved peering through the magical window to catch glimpses of Lizzy working. Her brown ponytail swished back and forth while she walked around the shop, constantly flitting from station to station.

Unfortunately, the ease with which she moved ended whenever Ethan entered her shop. They had finished their date on an awkward note that didn't look like it was going to resolve any time soon. He had tried to talk with her, but she was shutting him out just as effectively as she had in the beginning, except now Ethan knew what he was missing. He knew what it felt like to hold her in his arms, and to laugh alongside her.

He thought they were friends, which made the rejection sting even worse than before.

He was putting the final touch on the miniature Ethan's Crumbs display when he spied Lizzy crossing the street towards his shop. Her face was covered by a scarf, with only her eyes peering out above the fluffy yellow yarn. It was impossible to read her expression.

Ethan turned when the bell above the door chimed, a surge of anxiety rushing through his body. He pressed his palms against his legs, using the pressure to keep his breathing calm.

"Hi." Lizzy's voice was soft.

"Hi." His voice cracked, like a young man in junior high

getting up the courage to ask a cute girl to dance. Ethan was better than that. He cleared his throat.

"It's good to see you again. How have you been?"

Lizzy unwound her scarf, which meant she was planning to stay for more than a second. Ethan's heart began a hopeful patter in his chest. Maybe they could talk things out and find a solution to the Connie problem.

She lay the scarf on a chair and slipped out of her coat. "Do you have a minute?"

Ethan nodded. He would find the time for her, even if he was busy. Thankfully, the store was in a bit of a lull. He pulled out a chair for Lizzy to sit.

Lizzy gave him a small smile. "I'm sorry I've been radio silent since our date. Finding out who was trying to hurt the shops really messed with my emotions."

"It wasn't easy for me to see her either." The gut punch from finding Connie still smarted.

"I know." Lizzy twisted her hands together. "The thing is, I'm not good with uncomfortable situations. I think you've seen your fair share of that."

"Maybe just a little." Dozens of memories flitted through Ethan's mind. Lizzy hadn't exactly been warm to him when she found out they'd be competitors.

She leaned forward in her chair. "I was upset that you didn't want me to confront Connie. She is in the wrong, and we both know it."

Ethan nodded, afraid to say anything that would stop Lizzy's train of thought when she was finally opening up to him.

"The thing is, once I had the chance to cool down, I could see that you were right. I recognize that missing out on her chance at opening a brick-and-mortar store would be difficult. Food trucks are great, but they don't offer much by way of expansion."

"Are you ready to forgive her?"

Lizzy shook her head. "Not yet. But I'm also not eager to yell at her. I do think we need to have a talk, face to face. In fact, . . ." Lizzy trailed off to check her phone. "She's going to be here in ten minutes."

Ethan rubbed his ear. Surely, he was hearing things wrong. "You invited her here. To my shop?" Lizzy's words weren't making sense.

"I thought it would be good to talk to her together. You keep a much cooler head than I do."

Disbelief clouded Ethan's mind. Deciding to forgive Connie was a personal thing. The fact that Lizzy was choosing peace was great, but she hadn't bothered to ask how he felt. Maybe he wasn't ready to let it go.

"How can you spring something like this on me? You didn't give me any time to prepare. Besides, I don't want my customers walking in on a confrontation. This isn't my battle."

Lizzy pushed back from the table. "Oh, really? Because I'm pretty sure both of us were in those pictures. She was sabotaging your shop just as much as mine."

"Yeah, but I'm not the one who invited her over for an argument. We could have met at a neutral location."

The air in the room pressed down on Ethan, making it

difficult to breathe. "Why does she think she's coming here anyway?"

Lizzy ducked her head. "I told her she won a free box of cookies."

Ethan closed his eyes and pinched the bridge of his nose, trying to keep his breathing even. There were a few customers eating at the tables nearby. He wasn't going to give them something to gossip about.

"I'm only going to say this once. Please leave. If Connie shows up, I will send her your way. You can work out your arguments on your own time."

He braced himself for the explosion that was sure to come, but Lizzy was silent as she pulled on her coat. She wrapped the scarf around her face and walked out, pausing at the door. "I thought you wanted to be friends. If you were a real friend, you'd have my back."

With that, she swung the door open, letting in a blast of frigid air as she stormed out, taking with her Ethan's peace and quiet. She had brought a grenade into his store and left with the pin barely intact.

For a moment, Ethan was too stunned to speak. How could she speak of friendship when she so clearly didn't care about his feelings? If she had cared, she would have asked him how he felt about Connie instead of trying to force him to confront her.

In the end, it didn't matter how much he had enjoyed spending time with Lizzy. Ethan was smart enough to know when it was time to let go. He had a shop to run, and he hadn't been looking for a relationship to begin with. He would move on.

At least, that is what he told himself while he attached the final pieces to his window display. The window may not win the contest, but he was going to prove that he had what it took to stick around for the long haul. Lizzy could blow up her own career, but his cookies were here to stay.

CHAPTER 19

❆

*L*izzy's temper wasn't something she was proud of. She had been known to put her foot in her mouth, figuratively, at least a couple of times a week. The words always came out in a rush, and then, when she took the time to think about what she had said, the guilt followed.

There was no guilt, however, when it came to Ethan. She had thought they were a team, but him refusing to talk to Connie was a slap in the face. How were they going to solve anything if he wasn't willing to help her out?

The way things stood, she was going to have to solve the Connie problem on her own. The problem was, she didn't know what to say. It was one thing to accuse someone of trying to sabotage her shop. It was another thing, entirely, to be able to forgive the person who was in the wrong. Lizzy didn't want to say the wrong thing.

She paced back and forth in her shop, throwing glares

out the window towards Ethan's shop. How dare he leave her in a bind like that?

Maria watched Lizzy's movements, ducking her head whenever Lizzy caught her eye. Lizzy finally spun to face her. "Spit it out."

"What happened across the street? You look ready to spout flames."

The words were an accurate representation of how Lizzy felt. She spun a final time and headed behind the counter, scrubbing her hands at the sink before she picked up a spatula.

"You know we caught the woman taking pictures of us, right?"

Maria nodded. "Yeah." She had been on the stakeout in the tackle shop.

"We figured out who the lady actually is."

"You're kidding." Maria lowered the frosting bag she was holding. "Who is it?"

"She owns the doughnut truck. Or at least she works there."

"The one that usually parks near the library?" Maria licked her lips. "Those are the best doughnuts in town. Please don't tell me I'm going to have to start boycotting the truck."

Lizzy appreciated the loyalty. "I would never ask you to boycott anyone, but yes. That's the one."

"How did you figure it out?"

Maria was a perfect audience when Lizzy told her the story, gasping and sighing at all the right places. By the time Lizzy was done speaking, Robert had joined them too.

"I can't believe you guys didn't talk to her right then," Robert said. "I don't know that I would have been able to stay quiet."

"Well, that's about to change. I told her that she won a free box of cookies from Ethan's shop."

"If she's heading to Ethan's shop, what are you doing over here?" Maria piped a thin border of frosting around the edges of a gingerbread man cookie.

"He refused to go along with the plan."

"You told Ethan she was coming, right?" Robert asked.

"Yep. And like a coward, he's going to send her here." The fury was difficult to mask. "I thought he was going to be helpful."

"Why did he change his mind?" Maria asked.

The oven timer beeped, interrupting the conversation. Lizzy slid an oven mitt onto her hand and pulled out the piping hot tray, carefully setting it on the counter.

"He didn't know she was coming in the first place. I figured he'd appreciate my efforts and back me up."

Robert glanced at Maria, trying to hide a grimace.

"I saw that. What aren't you saying?" Lizzy refused to get upset with her employees, but the subtle glances back and forth told her they were hiding something.

"You didn't talk to Ethan first?" Maria asked. Her voice was calm, but her grip on the frosting bag was leaving dents.

"I didn't think I needed to. She hurt him, too."

Robert reached past her, setting the timer as he slid a new batch of cookies into the oven. "Did you have any sort of a plan? Or did you just spring the idea on him and expect him to know what to do?"

His words punched her to the core.

That was the problem. She hadn't asked Ethan for his advice before she reached out to Connie. She had just assumed he would back her up. But that wasn't how they had handled everything else. They had handled every other situation as a team.

The air whooshed out of her lungs, her anger deflating along with her pride. "Guys. I think I messed up."

Maria pointed out the window. "Well, you don't really have time to fix it. Isn't that the woman you showed us a picture of last week?"

Sure enough, Connie was waiting at the light, the scowl on her face easy to see. She was clearly not excited about having to cross the street.

Lizzy's phone chimed with a text.

She's all yours. Good luck.

The words cut deep. Lizzy had been holding onto a sliver of hope that Ethan would change his mind and run to her shop to help her talk to Connie, but he wasn't coming. She was going to have to do this on her own.

"Let's make her a box of cookies. I told her she won a free box and I'm guessing Ethan didn't give her one."

"Good call." Robert quickly slid four warm cookies into a lavender box, closing the lid with a smirk before he handed the box to Lizzy. "She really doesn't deserve these."

"Probably not, but I don't know what else to do."

When the door chimed a minute later, Lizzy was ready. She welcomed Connie to the store with a smile, determined to ignore the scowl on Connie's face.

"Thanks for coming," Lizzy said.

Connie waved her hand towards the street. "I was told to go to Ethan's Crumbs. Why was I given the wrong address?"

Lizzy pressed her hands to her sides, slowly exhaling so she could speak with a level voice. "That was my fault. I thought the three of us would be able to talk together, but I didn't confirm the location with Ethan first."

"Well. That doesn't seem very professional to me."

A few very unprofessional words ran through Lizzy's mind. Words that would land her in the confession box at church. She swallowed down her anger, refusing to engage in a fight.

"I'm sorry for the mix up, but I'm grateful you are here." Lizzy slid a box of cookies across the counter to Connie. "For starters, here's the cookies I said you won."

Connie flicked the lid of the box open, her thin lips cracking a slight smile. "Thanks." She turned to leave, but Lizzy ran past her and stepped in front of the door.

"Since you're here, can we talk?"

Connie gripped the box, her eyes narrowing to slits. "Why would you want to do that?"

Lizzy pulled out a chair for Connie and then sat on the opposite side of the table, waiting for Connie to join her.

"I think we both know how you feel about my shop. I'd like to clear the air."

Connie shrugged but didn't say anything as she sat down.

It wasn't an answer but at least the woman was staying. Lizzy crossed her fingers under the table, praying for a peaceful resolution. She decided to go with a diplomatic approach, instead of hurling accusations.

"Did I do something to offend you?" Lizzy kept her voice low so they wouldn't attract the attention of the customers at the tables nearby.

"Why would you ask that?" Connie flicked her hair over her shoulder, the picture of innocence.

Lizzy's stomach sank. If Connie was going to play dumb, there wasn't much she could do. She was going to have to be more direct.

"Connie, I'm pretty sure you are the one who has been posting pictures of me and Ethan online. We saw you taking them the other day."

That hit landed. Connie flinched. "It's a free world. I can take pictures of anything I want."

Lizzy's blood was starting to boil. Connie wasn't openly denying the pictures. Instead, she was acting like it was no big deal.

"Are you done taking pictures of us yet?" Lizzy's leg was bouncing like a jackhammer, but she was still trying to keep her voice low.

Connie pushed her chair back. "It depends. Are you ready to admit that you and Ethan are working together?"

"I'm not in the habit of lying. If I was secretly running a store with Ethan, why on earth would we choose to have double the overhead by paying for two shops? It doesn't make any sense, from either a business perspective or a basic point of logic."

"I never said you guys were being logical. But you must admit that the odds are pretty miniscule of you both opening shops during the same week if you weren't working together."

Lizzy forced her hands to unclench. "I thought it was pretty incredible, too. Believe me, if I had my way, his shop never would have opened."

Connie opened her eyes wide before smoothing out her expression. "Interesting. Are you saying you wish his shop would close?"

It was clear Connie was eager to twist whatever words Lizzy said. She was probably already mentally writing the next community post about how Lizzy hated Ethan and wanted to destroy his shop.

Lizzy gathered her thoughts before answering. "In the beginning, I was hoping his shop would fail. But now I've gotten to know the man."

She glanced out the window as she spoke, catching sight of his brown hair walking past the tall display. Just seeing his hair gave her stomach a little flutter. She knew she'd be crushed if his shop closed.

"The truth is, Ethan is a pretty incredible guy. Once I got to know him, I realized he's trying to follow his dreams just like I am. He wants his shop to succeed as much as I do. I'm not going to get in the way of that."

Thinking back on her first impression of Ethan was embarrassing. Lizzy had acted like a jealous monster, judging his every action without an ounce of kindness. Her actions from today felt a lot like the earlier days, but now she knew how much she liked him. She didn't have any time to waste with petty arguments.

Lizzy pushed back from the table, her quick movement causing a frown to appear on Connie's face.

"I thought you wanted to talk." Connie folded her arms across her chest defensively, her displeasure easy to read.

The patience Lizzy tried to cultivate was gone. "Here's the thing. I thought I'd be able to reason with you, person to person. The reality is, you're going to continue to post whatever you'd like to on the community page. I hope you can find it in your heart to forgive us for getting in the way of your dreams. For now, I have a fence I need to mend."

Lizzy threw her apron behind the counter and met Robert's eye. "I'll be back in ten."

"Good luck," he said.

The cold air bit into Lizzy's skin while she raced across the street, dodging cars in her hurry to get to Ethan's shop.

Kitty jumped when Lizzy barged in the door.

"Where's Ethan? I need to talk to him."

Kitty shrugged. "I think he left for the day."

The words doused Lizzy's heart. She was barely aware of Kitty confirming with Chad that Ethan was gone. Somehow, she managed to say goodbye and walk out the door without breaking down.

There wasn't any chance to fix the giant mess Lizzy had created in person. She sent a text to Ethan, begging him to hear her out, but he didn't respond. She headed back to her shop, her spirits low.

It was fitting that by the end of the day, a snowstorm had blown in, bringing flurries of snowflakes while the temperatures plummeted. Lizzy's slow drive home gave her plenty of time to think. By the time she was pulling into her garage, she still had no idea what to do.

Fixing this problem was going to take a lot more than a box of cookies.

CHAPTER 20

❄

*E*than was trying to play solitaire on his phone, but every time he picked it up, he was reminded of the text Lizzy sent, asking him to talk. Given her mood earlier in the day, Ethan was pretty sure that by talk she meant lecture, and he didn't have the energy for that.

He had been turning his cheek for months, trying to be the bigger person whenever Lizzy was upset. Time after time, he had met her temper with kindness. The truth was, he was exhausted. There was only so many times a man could be beaten down before he had to accept that things weren't how he wanted them to be.

Laying out all the facts, Ethan was crazy about Lizzy. He loved talking to her, and seeing the sparkle in her eye that lit up whenever she spoke. He could spend hours with her tucked under his arm, talking about whatever silly topic came to mind. He didn't even mind her fiery temper. It kept him on his toes.

The problem was trying to figure out what he meant to her. If there wasn't mutual respect in the relationship, was it worth pursuing? Ethan had made the mistake of giving away too much of himself in the past. He wasn't looking for another failed relationship.

It wasn't reasonable for her to expect him to agree with every decision she made. That wasn't how relationships worked. In fact, some of the strongest relationships he knew had two people who disagreed on numerous things, but their respect for each other let them work through their problems. If they didn't come to an agreement, at least they came up with a compromise.

Ethan threw his phone down on his bed, switching on a hockey game instead of feeling guilty about the unanswered message. Cindy curled up beside him. Absentmindedly petting her brought a pang to his heart. Cindy was a great pet, but she wasn't a replacement for human companionship. He had gotten a taste of what it felt like to snuggle with Lizzy, and that was what he craved.

By the time Ethan's team was down by three goals, he knew he needed a different distraction. He pulled his recipe books down from the cupboard above the stove, taking his time to scan each page until he found the perfect recipe to try. If he couldn't talk to Lizzy, at least he could bake his feelings away.

The first batch of cookies was done, and the second tray was in the oven, when the exhaustion finally set in. Ethan had already been on his feet for most of the day, and he knew the morning was going to come quickly.

Yawns were coming closer and closer together when Ethan washed the pans. He put the last cookie sheet on the rack to dry and headed to his room, half asleep. His heart was heavy when he plugged in his phone, still not knowing what to say to Lizzy.

* * *

SOMETIME IN THE middle of the night, the power went out. Ethan awoke to frozen toes and a phone with ten percent battery life. Getting out of bed was a test of his willpower, as was convincing himself that it was okay to cross the frigid floor to his closet for warmer clothes.

By the time he was ready for work, he was exhausted. It was tempting to call in sick, but he was the boss. How could he expect his employees to treat the job seriously if he wasn't willing to act the same?

On his drive to work, it became clear that a large section of houses were without power. He felt bad for the families that had to get children off to school. It was going to be a rough day for a lot of his neighbors. If there were leftover cookies, Ethan was sure his neighbors would appreciate something to cheer up their families.

Ethan pulled on to Main Street, relieved to see that the power was still on. He didn't think he could handle another day of being shut down.

It was habit now to glance over at Lizzy's shop. He could see the employees inside, hard at work. Based on the flurry of activity inside, Ethan guessed they were hoping for a big day of sales. He circled around the back of his shop and forced his thoughts to focus on the day ahead.

Sarah was the first of his employees to arrive. Ethan was relieved. He knew if Kitty was working, he'd be getting grilled. With Sarah, it was easy to focus on the work they had to do rather than gossip about Ethan's non-existent love life and the way his heart twinged every time he thought about Lizzy.

His peace lasted until right before opening time, when Kitty barged into the shop, her scarf still wound around her neck.

"The voting is over. Do you think Lizzy won?" Kitty's exuberance was how Ethan should have been feeling.

"I'm not sure. I hope so." He tried to infuse excitement into his voice, but it didn't fool anyone.

"Why aren't you more excited for her?" Kitty planted her hands on her hips, staring him down. "Are you guys still fighting?"

Ethan shook his head. "She needs some space. It's fine."

The words were enough to slow Kitty's questions, but they left Ethan feeling unsettled. He was avoiding the shop because he wasn't sure what Lizzy's reaction to him would be. Their last interaction had ended in harsh words. He wasn't eager for a repeat performance.

Ethan was refilling the flour container when the doorbell chimed. When he saw who was entering the shop, his heart dropped. The last thing he needed was a confrontation. He slid a lid on top of the container and wiped his hands on his apron before approaching the counter.

"Hi, Connie."

She studied the menu, taking her time to look at each flavor even though there were only a few to choose from. Ethan's stomach was rolling, but he kept a smile plastered on his face.

Finally, after a line started to form behind her, she began to speak. "Which cookies go best with an apology? I owe you a big one."

Ethan moved to the end of the counter so he could talk to Connie uninterrupted. "You don't need to buy my cookies to apologize."

"I know, but I figured it would help break the ice." Connie pressed her hands to the countertop. "I am here to apologize for all the things I've been saying about you. I was mad about the shops being sold, and I took it out on you and Lizzy. I'm sorry."

Ethan opened his mouth for the standard reply, but stopped to think about if he could really accept her apology.

"I think, more than anything, I'm confused about why you took so much time to follow me and Lizzy. Friendship is complicated enough without someone trying to ruin it."

Connie nodded. "I know. Lizzy helped me to see how wrong I had been."

That was news to Ethan. It was encouraging to know that Lizzy had managed to get through a talk with Connie without blowing everything up. If she could forgive Connie, maybe she'd eventually forgive him.

"I really appreciate you coming by. I can't do anything

about the way you treated me in the past, but I hope we can start fresh moving forward."

"I'd like that. Lizzy told me what an incredible guy you are. I wasn't sure I believed her, but I'm glad she said something. I'd like to be friends with both of you."

Ethan thanked Connie and watched her leave, his mind spinning. Lizzy had said kind things about him, but he didn't know if he could trust any of them. He needed space to figure out where her mind was really at.

By closing time, Ethan was no closer to figuring out his heart. He went home, purposefully driving the long way around so he wouldn't see Lizzy's shop. His heart couldn't handle seeing her brown ponytail bouncing around the store.

The power was on when he got back home. He was grateful for the warmth. At least, at the end of a long day, he could curl up with Cindy.

Ethan was drifting off to sleep in front of the television when a call startled him awake. He stared at the phone, a sense of dread filling his stomach. If he flipped the phone over and the screen said Lizzy, would he be brave enough to answer?

It was easier to ignore the phone entirely. If it was important, the person could leave a message. He let it go to voicemail.

The phone stopped ringing, only to start again a second later. Ethan let it go to voicemail again. He wasn't in the head space to talk to anyone.

The third time the phone started ringing, Ethan realized that maybe it was important. He flipped the phone over, his stomach lightening at the sight of his best friend Tate's number.

"Hey, man. What's up?"

Tate's voice broke as he spoke, and Ethan's stomach plummeted. "What's going on?"

"It's Thomas, man. He's in the hospital."

Lead poured through Ethan's veins. "What happened?" Thomas and Ethan had been roommates until Thomas got married. The last Ethan had heard, he was in great shape.

"He lost control when going down the slopes. He's alive, but his leg is toast. They're taking him into surgery soon."

"What do you need me to do?"

"Right now?" Tate's voice broke. "I think right now all we can do is pray for him, man. It's going to be a rough road for him."

"I can do that." Ethan thanked Tate and hung up the phone, all desire for sleep gone. He was frantic for a way to help. Prayers were great, but he wanted more.

After a restless night of sleep, Ethan had a plan. He headed to work armed with two printed signs. *For every cookie purchased today, we'll make a donation to the Thomas Castelle hospital fund.*

He hung one on the door and taped one to the register. His hope was that people would buy an extra cookie or two. He planned to send the profits from the day to help with Thomas's hospital bills. It wouldn't be a lot, but every bit would help.

Once the shop opened, it became clear that people were

curious about Thomas's condition. Ethan printed out a photo of Thomas giving a thumbs up from his hospital bed. His friend's face was bruised, and his leg was in a sling, but he still managed to look upbeat.

During the morning rush, almost everyone purchased an extra cookie. The purchasing slowed in the late afternoon. Ethan couldn't figure out why. The signs hadn't changed. He figured maybe people were just more generous in the mornings for some reason.

He was helping a group of teenage boys when he heard the gossip.

"I already donated to this guy." The teenager flipped his hair back and reached for his cookie. "I hope he gets better soon."

That was news to Ethan. As far as he knew, he was the only person in town who had ever met Thomas.

"Where did you donate?" Ethan asked.

"The other cookie shop."

Ethan could barely keep a smile on his face while he finished the transaction. He couldn't believe Lizzy's nerve. It was one thing to fight for the same customers. It was something else entirely to steal donations from his friend.

He was stuck in the shop until closing time, but each customer left him a little more upset. From what he could gather, there was a large box set up in Lizzy's shop labeled "Donations for Thomas". People were proud to have donated, but each time they told him they did, his pulse sped up.

He didn't know why Lizzy had stolen his idea, and he

was going crazy not being able to ask. She was trying to sabotage his donations. There had to be a mistake, because even Lizzy wouldn't stoop that low.

Ethan hurried through the clean-up, eager to march over to Lizzy's shop and demand an answer. He was mopping the floor when a knock on the window made him look up. Lizzy stood on the sidewalk; her cheeks red with cold. In her arms, she held a large box.

CHAPTER 21

❄

*L*izzy's hands were shaking as she stood in front of Ethan's store. The last time she had spoken to him, she had been incredibly rude. She hoped that her donation would help soften the blow.

Ethan's face was angry when he opened the door.

"Can I come in?" Lizzy held the box out as a peace offering.

He shook his head. "I don't need cookies. And honestly, I'm not sure I want to talk."

Patching things up was going to be more difficult than Lizzy thought. "This isn't a box of cookies. It's a donation for Thomas."

Ethan's eyes widened, but he quickly regained composure. "I guess you'd better come in."

There was a chill in the air when Lizzy walked into the shop. She was used to feeling like a guest. Now she felt like an intruder. She wasn't sure how to fix things with Ethan, but she knew she had to try. The box in her hands was a start.

She held it out again, and this time, Ethan took the box.

"I'm confused." He held the box to his side, not opening the flap. "Why did you decide to donate?"

Lizzy toyed with the edge of her scarf. "I don't think I'd realized how many people cross between our shops. I was helping a mom and her kids who had already been to your store. She asked me if I was taking donations."

"So you decided you'd start collecting money? That's messed up."

"She assumed we were friends because of the community posts. She didn't want to drag her kids back across the street, so she asked me to bring the cash to you next time I saw you. The man in line behind her heard our conversation. He wanted to donate, too, so I put out a box."

Ethan's expression didn't change when slid the box onto the table. He opened the lid and his mouth dropped open.

"How much money is in here?"

"I stopped counting, but I'm guessing there's easily $700 in there."

"And that's all from donations today?"

"I couldn't believe it. Customers would ask who Thomas was, but I didn't know what to say. I told them he was one of your friends. Is he?"

Ethan cleared his throat but his voice still broke. "He is one of my best friends. He was in a pretty bad skiing accident yesterday."

Lizzy's heart ached for Ethan. It was never fun to watch someone you cared about be in pain. She placed a hand on his arm, half expecting Ethan to pull away.

"Is he going to be okay?"

A shrug was the only answer Ethan gave, but it was enough to break down the man's rough walls. He pulled out a chair and slumped down, pushing the donation box to the center of the table.

It was a calculated risk to sit in a chair next to Ethan, but Lizzy pulled it out, trying to leave a little space between their bodies. It would be natural to wrap her arms around him, but the timing wasn't right. Instead, Lizzy slid her hand close to his. She hoped he'd feel her comfort.

The shift in Ethan's body was almost imperceptible, but Lizzy held still. Before long, his pinky finger was resting next to hers, skin to skin. Tingles raced up her arm, warming her body.

She took a breath and lifted her finger, wrapping it around his. The corner of his mouth lifted into a small smile.

The situation really wasn't about Lizzy and Ethan's relationship, but she had come for a reason. She covered his hand with hers. "Ethan, I've been awful to you. I know you've got heavy things on your mind, but I'd love to be there for you. I don't want to be just friends. I want so much more."

His cheek lifted with a genuine smile. When he turned his full gaze on Lizzy, she had to remind herself to stay present in the moment. It would be easy to get swept away in his ocean blue eyes.

He gave her hand a gentle squeeze and Lizzy leaned forward. This was the moment she was waiting for. He was going to kiss her, and everything would be right with the world. Instead, he let go pushed his chair back.

"It's been a long day. Can we talk tomorrow?"

Lizzy nodded and headed for the door, trying to hold her disappointment inside. Her hand was on the handle when Ethan called out to her.

"Hey Lizzy?"

Tears were welling up in her eyes, so she didn't turn around. "Yeah, Ethan?"

"Thanks again for the donation."

"You're welcome." With that, Lizzy pulled the door open and stepped onto the sidewalk. Cold air stung her eyes, the final catalyst before her tears began to fall.

It didn't make sense to be upset. Lizzy hadn't been looking for a relationship. She had her priorities, and dating Ethan didn't logically fit into the picture. At least, that's what she told herself while she headed back to her shop.

She was crossing the street when a chill ran up her spine. The winter daylight hours were short, which meant that the streetlights were already flickering on. In the dim light, she could see a group of people waiting outside.

Her mind flashed back to the men who had been loitering the night Ethan came to save her. They had shared their first kiss that night, but it didn't erase the danger that they had been in before the kiss. Lizzy had no way to know that moment would be the start of their relationship. Now she ached to make things right.

The temptation to turn back to Ethan's shop for help was strong, but he had made his feelings clear. If she was going to be an independent woman, she'd have to deal with the situation on her own.

Lizzy headed towards her shop, her trepidation turning to curiosity when she got closer. The people didn't appear to be drunk. In fact, they were talking animatedly with each other.

Lizzy approached the people from the side, startling a thin woman in a bright yellow peacoat.

The woman jumped but a smile spread across her face. "She's here!"

In response, all the faces turned towards Lizzy. She studied them, trying to figure out what was going on. One of the men looked vaguely familiar, but Lizzy couldn't place him.

He stretched out his hand. "We were hoping to catch you before you went home. I wanted to be the first to congratulate you on winning the window decorating contest. The camera crews will be by tomorrow morning, and I'll be there to present your check."

The pieces were clicking into place. This was the mayor and what Lizzy guessed were some of his staff.

"I won?" Her thoughts were swirling.

"You did. We won't officially announce it until tomorrow, but I know people like to be ready for their photo ops.

Your cookie shop is about to be plastered across the community page. I hope you're ready for more business."

The surprise of the situation took a minute to kick in. "Thank you. I'm honored."

The mayor shook her hand. "Thanks for making downtown a special place to be. Your efforts were appreciated."

He said goodbye, leaving a stunned Lizzy standing in the street.

The goal had been to win the window decorating contest, but the competition had been tight. Getting in the top three was an honor but she hadn't thought she'd win. Her first thought was to run back to Ethan's shop and share the good news. Instead, she pulled out her phone and called Maisy, holding her phone away from her ear when her sister started cheering.

Maisy kept Lizzy entertained until it was time to head home. The day had been long, and even though Lizzy was excited, there was a heaviness in her heart that wouldn't go away. She couldn't wait to get off her feet and snuggle up in bed with her book, forgetting all about her worries for a few hours.

A beat-up car was waiting in front of Lizzy's house when she pulled up. Even with the loud engine off, Lizzy knew who the car belonged to. The street was dark, but there was enough light to see a silhouette of the man behind the steering wheel.

Lizzy's heart began a hopeful beat in her chest. Ethan wouldn't be in front of her house unless he had made a decision. If the decision was to stay friends, he would have no reason to come over. The alternative made sense. He was going to give their relationship a try.

The garage door took forever to open. All Lizzy wanted was to talk to Ethan, but she wasn't going to leave her car in the driveway. She pulled the car into the garage and turned off the engine, suddenly self-conscious. What if she was wrong?

She climbed out of her car and turned. When she saw Ethan walking towards her, a large vase of flowers in his hands, all her fears went away. She stepped towards him, meeting him at the mouth of the garage.

"I thought you'd already be home," he said. "I was worried you'd gone somewhere else."

Lizzy shook her head. "I had to take care of something at work. Would you like to come in?"

"Yes, please." Ethan handed her the vase. "These are for you."

He didn't say anything else as he followed Lizzy into the house, but she could feel the weight of his stare on her back. They walked to the kitchen and Lizzy put the flowers on the counter.

"They're beautiful." In the light, she could admire the deep red of the roses, with white daisies scattered throughout.

Ethan slid his hands in and out of his coat pockets, clearly uncomfortable. Lizzy decided to help him out of his misery.

"I'm glad to see you, but why are you here? I thought you needed space."

He straightened the front of his coat. "It took about two minutes after you left for me to realize that I hadn't given you the answer I wanted to."

Hope bloomed in Lizzy's chest. "And what answer would that be?"

"I want to be with you. The time I've gotten to know you has certainly been a whirlwind. We've had some good highs and more than enough really deep lows. I don't want to be the guy on the other side of the street who watches your life go by, sitting on the sidelines. I want to be part of every step."

Tears brimmed in Lizzy's eyes, making it difficult to speak. "That's what I want, too, but I'm afraid I'll mess things up. My fiery personality is something I'm working on. I know I need to change. I just don't know how."

Ethan slid his hands around her waist. "I don't need you to change who you are. You are the woman I'm crazy about, fiery personality and all. We may need to work on our communication skills, but every relationship does."

Every word he said was a balm to Lizzy's soul. He liked her for who she was. "But what if I mess things up again?"

Ethan winked. "I'm pretty sure you will, but so will I. I personally am a fan of the kiss and make up part of dating."

With that, he closed the gap between them, pressing his lips to hers with a kiss that left no room for misunderstandings. Lizzy let herself get carried away, her heart thumping erratically as she kissed him back.

There was no need for words, but Ethan pulled back, kissing her forehead before he grabbed her hands. "In case you didn't understand, yes, I want you. Rough patches and all. I want to keep exploring all there is to know about you. I don't want to waste another day wondering if we could make it work."

He kissed her again, slowing the kiss so that tingles raced from the top of Lizzy's head to the tips of her toe as she hungrily pressed her lips to his.

This time, Lizzy was the first to break their embrace. "I definitely like the kiss and make up part, too, but we need to talk."

Ethan's eyes widened, but he nodded. "Should we sit down?"

Lizzy led the way to the couch, waiting for Ethan to sit so she could curl up by his side. He draped his arm across her shoulder as if it were the most natural thing in the world to do, but his leg tapped a beat that said he wasn't completely comfortable.

"What do you want to talk about?"

Lizzy eyed Ethan's bouncing leg, his nerves rubbing off on her. "I won the contest."

She glanced up to see his expression. Words were easy to cloak under a tone of positivity, but his body language would tell her what he was really feeling.

The smile that beamed across his face looked genuine, as did the squeeze of her shoulders. "I hoped you would."

Ethan pressed a kiss to her forehead, but Lizzy's heart was heavy. "They are coming to present the check tomorrow. By tomorrow afternoon, my name is going to be advertised all over the community page."

"I know." Ethan trailed kisses down the side of her forehead, stopping to nuzzle her ear.

It was difficult to think with him distracting her. Pushing away felt impossible, but Lizzy scooted to the next cushion. "Ethan." She pressed her hand to his knee. "My only goal when I met you was to figure out a way to put your shop out of business."

"Yeah. I wasn't a fan of that, even though I was secretly hoping to do the same to yours." Ethan covered her hand with his. "But we've moved past that, right? At least, I know I have."

Lizzy thoughts were swirling. "The problem is that I don't want your shop to fail anymore, but I'm afraid that with all the good press coming my way, we aren't playing on a level field anymore."

Ethan raised his eyebrows. "So, you think you're going to push me out of business?"

Her stomach was sinking. "It's not that. I just—".

A smile danced across Ethan's mouth while he held a finger to her lips. "There are always risks in business. I am going to do everything in my power to make my shop a success, but if it goes under, I will adapt. I don't want to worry about the future that may or may not happen."

"That's not being realistic." Lizzy's shoulders were tensing. "I don't want to lose you over this."

Ethan stood up, causing a wave of worry to crash over Lizzy's body. He had been incredibly sweet, but he could see her logic. There really wasn't room for a relationship.

He held his hand out, and Lizzy let him pull her to her

feet. "I am only going to say this once, so I want you to listen carefully."

The blue eyes were smoldering. Ethan slid his hand to Lizzy's waist. "I do not care if my shop goes under."

She shook her head. "You don't mean that." His shop meant too much to him.

"I wasn't finished." Ethan slid his other hand to her shoulder, playing with a strand of her hair. "I'm going to do everything in my power to make sure you have competition for your shop for years to come. Winning the contest will give you a boost this year, but I already have ideas for next year's contest. I don't plan to give up on my shop, or on my relationship with you."

Lizzy's heart was beating fast. "That sounds perfect to me. I can't wait to beat you again next year."

"We'll see."

With that, Ethan lowered his head to kiss Lizzy again. This kiss was short, but it held a promise that took Lizzy's breath away. She couldn't wait to see their future unfold.

CHAPTER 22

❄

*E*than stood in the crowd, his hood up and his scarf wrapped to cover half of his face. He didn't want to draw any attention to himself, but he didn't need to worry. All eyes were turned to Lizzy, standing in a red coat in front of her store. She was radiant when she accepted her check from the mayor.

Part way into her thank you speech, Lizzy made eye contact with Ethan. "I couldn't have done it without the support of some really great friends."

Her words warmed him to the core. Only the two of them knew that there was a deep romance brewing beneath that friendship. They were keeping it quiet until after the spotlight was off Lizzy's shop.

A round of applause accompanied the end of Lizzy's short speech. Her broad smile reflected the pride she felt at doing a good job. Lizzy's employees joined her in front of the store for photo ops. Chad cocked an eyebrow at Ethan, obviously recognizing him, but he quickly smoothed his face for the camera.

That was Ethan's clue to leave. He slid to the back of the crowd and then crossed the street, walking behind the buildings to enter his shop from the rear. No one noticed him leaving, which was exactly how he wanted it to be.

Hours later, after the cookie shops were closed, Ethan walked hand in hand with Lizzy through a grocery store. "Are you sure they sell hot cocoa here?" He was teasing Lizzy but her face turned down in a frown.

"I thought they did." She stopped in the middle of the aisle, cutting off a man who was pushing his cart behind them.

"Sorry, sir." Ethan smiled apologetically before he slid Lizzy out of the way. He reached for her hand. "You seem distracted. What's on your mind?"

"I was thinking about this morning. Did you see Connie there?"

Ethan hadn't paid any attention to the crowd. He was too busy keeping his chin down, trying to blend in. "I didn't notice her. Did she come?"

"Yeah. I was surprised she showed up."

The muscles in Ethan's stomach clenched. "Do you think she's planning another smear campaign?" He was going to be furious if Connie tried to take the spotlight from Lizzy. Lizzy deserved all the praise she was getting.

She rubbed her thumb back and forth along the edge of his hand. "I don't think she's going to cause any more trouble. It felt like we got to a good place when we talked."

"Did I tell you she apologized to me?" Ethan wasn't sure if it was wise to bring her up.

Lizzy dropped his hand and stepped forward to wrap him in a hug.

"I know we've talked through a lot of things." Her hand danced along Ethan's back. "I really am sorry about the way I handled Connie. That wasn't fair to you."

The way Lizzy's head rested perfectly against his chest made it difficult for Ethan to speak. He smoothed down her hair, not wanting to ruin the moment by saying something insensitive. The ability to talk about difficult subjects was important to him, so he decided to be honest.

"I knew, when we were getting back together, that there would be things we didn't agree on." Ethan tilted Lizzy's chin up so he could look into her eyes. "The situation with Connie is a perfect example of that. I wish I had handled myself better. I was caught off guard."

"Because I sprang her on you." Lizzy's voice dropped to an exaggerated whisper. "I don't know if you know this, but sometimes, I act irrationally."

Ethan laughed, pulling her down the aisle towards the cocoa cans. "Really? I hadn't noticed."

"Even though she went about everything the wrong way, I wish there was something we could do to help her."

Ethan's heart was filled with admiration for Lizzy. "Your desire to help others is one of the many things I love about you."

"You love me?" Lizzy's eyes sparkled; her mouth lifted into a teasing smirk.

"I didn't say that." As the words left his lips, Ethan realized that he didn't want to waste another day holding back the words he felt.

"What is love anyway? Other than a word?" The air in the store closed Ethan and Lizzy in a small bubble. "Lizzy Thompson, I am smitten by you. If love means never wanting to spend another day apart, then yes, I love you. I don't expect you to feel the same way, yet, but I hope you get there."

Lizzy lifted a finger to shush him. "You don't really fit into my life plan. School. Shop. Then a relationship. But you've surprised me in all the best ways. I love you, too."

There wasn't room in Ethan's chest to hold the joy he felt hearing those simple words. He sealed their words with a gentle kiss before walking hand in hand down the aisle with the woman he loved.

* * *

THE LAST FEW weeks of December passed in a blur. Ethan spent long hours in the shop, working overtime to keep up with the orders. Every evening he'd cross the street to pick up Lizzy or she'd come to his shop to wait for him. It became a game to see who could close their shop the quickest.

Watching Lizzy walk through his door was one of Ethan's favorite parts of the day. Her cheeks were always red from the cold, but her eyes sparkled.

On Christmas Eve, Ethan closed the shop early. He said

it was because he wanted all his employees to be able to spend time with their families, but he had an ulterior motive. He was looking forward to an entire evening alone with Lizzy.

A quick glance into her shop showed her bustling back and forth, serving each customer with a smile. When she flipped her sign to say closed, Ethan's heart began to race. He still had a couple of things to finish before he could enjoy his time off.

Ethan turned on the cocoa machine to fill two cups to the brim with steaming cocoa. He snapped on each lid, grateful for the insulation that would keep their drinks warm until they were ready for them.

With the cocoa ready, all that remained was cleaning the rest of the shop. Ethan took his time so Lizzy could beat him. He had a surprise date planned for the afternoon, but he needed Lizzy to be in his shop for the start of it.

Ethan kept an eye on Lizzy's shop until she walked out the front door, turning to lock it behind her. That was his cue. He texted a number he had saved in his phone.

It's time.

After the thumbs up came through, Ethan pulled on his coat. He opened the door to greet Lizzy with a kiss.

"You look ready to go," she said. She patted his coat. "What do you want to do with the rest of our day?"

Ethan pulled Lizzy in for a hug before releasing her. "I have a few things in mind." He walked behind the counter and grabbed the cocoa cups.

Lizzy took hers with a smile. "I can't wait."

"Follow me." Ethan led Lizzy outside, officially locking his shop until the day after Christmas. He looked down the street, pointing in the direction of jingling bells.

"I believe that's our ride," he said. Two chestnut brown horses appeared, their manes tied with red and gold ribbons. They were pulling a large, red sleigh with golden bells attached to the front.

Lizzy grabbed his hand. "Is that for us?"

"It is." Ethan waited until the sleigh had come to a stop. He waved to the driver before helping Lizzy to climb in, handing her cup up to her.

The driver greeted them with a grin. "It looks like we're in for a touch of snow. There are blankets to wrap yourself in if you get cold."

Ethan's heart was filled with gratitude when Lizzy snuggled next to his side, looping her arm through his.

"How did you think of this?" Her nose and cheeks were already turning red.

Ethan wrapped his arm around her shoulder so he could keep her warm. "I asked my friend what some of the best things to do in town were. He said a sleigh ride to the ranch was his favorite."

The wind blew across the open top of the sleigh, but Ethan appreciated the chance it gave him to hold Lizzy close. "Are you warm enough?"

Lizzy looked at his face. "Everything but my lips. They could use some warming up."

That was a task Ethan was prepared to handle. He tucked a strand of hair behind her ear, holding her gaze before he lowered his lips to hers. Kissing her softly, he pulled the blankets closer to her chin.

The ride through town felt magical, with snow gently falling around them while they looked at the various store windows. Ethan smiled when they turned off Main Street onto a country road. Rows of trees lined the road, their branches heavy with snow.

A curve in the road brought them to a slatted brown fence that stretched into the distance, lit with small white Christmas lights. Looming ahead of them was a red barn, the doors wide open. Tall pine trees flanked the doors, the branches decorated with red tinsel and golden ornaments.

Ethan helped Lizzy out of the sleigh. "Are you ready?"

"I have no idea what we're doing, but as long as I'm with you, it doesn't matter." She clasped his hand and Ethan felt like the luckiest man on the ranch.

Together, they headed towards the barn. The inside opened up to display a wood dance floor, with couples line dancing in time with an upbeat song.

"How are you at country dancing?" Ethan asked.

Lizzy unwound her scarf and slipped out of her coat, setting them on an empty chair. "I can keep up if I have a good leader."

Ethan added his warm clothes to the pile and pulled Lizzy to the center of the room. "Challenge accepted."

They watched the dancers for a few measures before joining in. Ethan tripped over his own feet a couple of times, but quickly picked up the steps. He was laughing by the time the song ended.

The music over the speakers switched to a slow song, and couples began to pair off. "Ready?" Ethan cupped a hand around Lizzy's waist, swaying in time with the two-step.

Laughter bubbled out of her. "I hope so."

None of their dance moves would win a championship, but Ethan had fun guiding Lizzy across the floor. When the song ended, he took a minute to study her face. Her flushed cheeks and bright eyes said she was ready for more.

Instead of another song, a man in a red vest walked to the front of the room. "Hey everyone. Thanks for being here. How does everyone feel about a surprise guest?"

Ethan and Lizzy cheered with the rest of the crowd.

"He's come all the way from the North Pole, stopping in to say hi before he heads off to work tonight. Let's give it up for Santa."

The crowd erupted into cheers as a plump Santa walked into the room wearing a red checkered shirt, a white leather vest, a cowboy hat, and boots with spurs.

Ethan had never seen a country Santa before, but the man fit in with the feel of the barn perfectly. The announcer waited until the cheering died down before gesturing to the corner where a chair covered in black and white cow print sat in front of a decorated tree.

"Feel free to visit with Santa for the rest of the evening. He hopes none of you have made his naughty list this year. Enjoy!"

With that, the music started up again. Ethan leaned

over to whisper in Lizzy's ear. "How about we keep our little store battles a secret?"

She threw her head back and laughed. "No way. I may not have acted the best but look where I ended up. I have my arm wrapped around the most handsome man in the room. I wouldn't change that for anything."

Ethan kissed her before pulling her back into a slow two-step around the room. "Are you sure about that?" He swung her close to the line. "Because I think we should meet Santa."

Lizzy nodded her head. "Only if we can get a picture with him. I'm going to hang it in the shop."

Standing in line, Ethan knew he'd chosen the right place for their date. He waited in line while Lizzy sat on Santa's lap, but she quickly waved him forward. "I already made my wish."

After smiling for photos, Ethan led Lizzy back onto the dance floor. "Do you want to tell me your wish?"

Lizzy shook her head. "If I tell you, it won't come true."

"Well, I didn't sit on Santa's lap so I can tell you what my wish would have been." Ethan pulled Lizzy closer, stroking the back of her hair.

She closed her eyes and rested her head on his chest.

"My wish would be that we can still be dancing together like this next year. I want to keep exploring my relationship with you. I hope that even with how busy our shops are, we can always find time to be together."

Lizzy pushed back from Ethan's chest, causing him to

wonder what he did wrong. "Were you listening to my super-secret Santa wish?"

Ethan shook his head. "No. Why?"

"Because." Lizzy stepped on her tiptoes to kiss his lips. "I asked Santa for the exact same thing."

EPILOGUE

The following Christmas -

Lizzy squirted frosting onto a cookie, absentmindedly spreading it with a spatula while she watched the clock counting down the minutes until the window decorating contest closed. As the winner of the previous year's contest, she was going to get to hear about this year's winner first.

Ethan's shop had made it to the final three. His window decorations from last winter were cute, but together they had added movement and some bright colors that pushed it over the edge. If everything went according to plan, he'd be the one getting the large check from the mayor.

A commotion outside caught her attention. Ethan was struggling with a large package, balancing it on one arm while he tried to open the door with his other. As she watched, the package wobbled back and forth before falling to the ground.

She raced outside the door, stepping onto the sidewalk so she could yell to her boyfriend. "Are you doing okay over there?"

Ethan laughed. "I've got it. I'll see you after work."

Over the past year, Ethan and Lizzy had shared everything, from experimenting with new recipes to kisses in the moonlight. Her Christmas wish had been that Santa would let her spend every day with Ethan, and so far, he had delivered.

The shrill ringing of her phone drew her attention. Lizzy held the receiver to her ear, letting out a loud whoop when the mayor told her the good news.

She wasn't supposed to tell Ethan he had won, but she could give him a congratulatory kiss without telling him what it was for. Lizzy strolled across the street, schooling her features into a small frown so she wouldn't give anything away. She opened the door, scanning the baking area for the large box. It was nowhere in sight.

"What were you carrying earlier?" she asked, greeting him with a kiss.

Ethan ducked his head, avoiding her eyes. "It's nothing. Just more supplies for the shop. Do you want to see?"

She got the distinct impression that he was hiding something but then he took her to the storage room. A large box sat in the center of the shelf.

"I don't know if I'll win the window contest, but I got these just in case." Dozens of smaller boxes sat inside the large one. Ethan pulled one out and flipped the lid open, displaying a carton filled with jingle bells. "I thought it would be cute to have bells sitting beside the register for customers to take in celebration of our win."

His face turned serious. "That is, if I win."

It took all of Lizzy's will power to say nothing. He was going to find out the good news soon enough.

She reached for his hand. "That is an adorable idea. Win or lose, you know I'll be cheering for you. Are we still on for tonight?"

They had gotten tickets to a Christmas concert that later that evening, and Lizzy couldn't wait to go. She loved seeing people singing and dancing. If the rumors were right, the entertainers danced through the audience, interacting with the crowd. The show was supposed to be uplifting and entertaining.

Ethan brushed his hair out of his eyes. "I'm planning on it. Do you want to dress up or go casual?"

"Dressy, please." Lizzy had picked out the perfect dress for Christmas parties earlier that month and hadn't found a chance to wear it yet.

"I'll dust off my tie."

* * *

The evening started with dinner at an upscale restaurant. Between the music and the low lights, the ambiance was incredibly romantic.

Lizzy was lifting a spoonful of soup to her mouth when the woman at the table next to her let out a small shriek before she began to cry.

A quick glance at the table made it clear what the commotion was all about. A well-dressed man knelt on the ground, holding out a small box. All eyes were on him as he pulled out a ring and slid it onto the woman's finger.

Lizzy cheered along with the rest of the patrons, but she couldn't help but feel a little pang of jealousy. She had everything she wanted in her relationship with Ethan. He was kind when she was brash. He smoothed out her rough edges and made her want to be a better person. All her future dreams included Ethan by her side.

The couple at the table next to them embraced before settling back into their chairs.

"That was sweet," Lizzy said.

Ethan's eyes sparkled when he reached for her hand. "I wonder if she had a set of rules he had to follow before he was allowed to propose."

"Are you making fun of my life plan?" When Lizzy made her plans, she hadn't expected to meet someone like Ethan. He had snuck up on her, making her dreams even bigger than she could have ever predicted.

"Maybe just a little bit. You made it so hard for me to officially date you." He kissed the back of her hand, sending a zing of electricity that shot through her body.

"I'm glad you persevered. This past year would've been so boring without you in my life." Lizzy snuck another glance at the happy couple. The woman's eyes were bright with tears while she held a phone to her ear. No doubt she was filling in her family about the big news.

She glanced at Ethan. He was watching the couple as well, the expression on his face difficult to read.

"Would you want to be proposed to somewhere public like that?" He smoothed down his shirt. "I always wonder how the woman feels, getting put on the spot with everyone watching. What if she wanted to say no?"

Lizzy's heart began to race. The tone in his voice suggested that he wasn't just asking a hypothetical question. She took her time to answer, even though she had been dreaming about her answer for months.

"I guess, if the guy was the right one, I wouldn't care how or where he proposed. Unless we were skydiving. I don't want to be proposed to while I'm scared out of my mind."

"What if you weren't ready?" Ethan's eyes were definitely not meeting hers.

Lizzy caressed his cheek. "If he was at the point of proposing, and I didn't feel strongly about him, I wouldn't still be with the guy. It seems cruel to drag someone along."

The grin that beamed across Ethan' face brought a new round of flutters. Lizzy could imagine the weight of a ring on her finger. All the way through dinner, and into dessert, Lizzy's mind wandered. She wondered how he would pop the question.

As much as Lizzy loved the idea of a wildly romantic proposal, she knew she didn't care what he ended up doing. Her dream was to spend eternity with the man she loved. The way he asked her wouldn't change that.

Only a few morsels of chocolate cake were left on the

plate when Ethan pushed his chair back. "We'd better go if we want to make the concert."

Lizzy was reluctant to leave their bubble. It was so easy to forget that other people were around when she was with Ethan. She followed him out the door, nestling against his side when the frigid air blasted against her.

The theater had a line of people waiting to get in. Lizzy tried to hold back her concern when the tickets that Ethan held out were rejected. The young girl at the counter looked up, confusion written across her face.

"I'm going to need to find a manager," she said. She scampered off, leaving Ethan and Lizzy at the counter with a rapidly growing line behind them.

"This is crazy," Lizzy said. "I knew the show was popular, but I had no idea it would be this busy. I'm impressed you got tickets."

"Me too." Ethan's hand rubbed a circle down her back, bringing warmth to her skin. "I wonder what the holdup is."

His question was answered a few minutes later when the girl came back with a manager trailing behind her.

"Can I see your tickets?" he asked.

Ethan handed the tickets over before pressing a kiss to the top of Lizzy's head. After a moment of furiously typing on a keyboard, the manager looked up.

"I'm so sorry, but it appears that there was some sort of computer glitch. Someone else also booked those seats. They have already been seated."

This was not how the evening was supposed to go. Lizzy's heart had been set on the concert, but it was looking like her date with Ethan was about to be cut short.

"We could try for another day," she said.

The manager shook his head. "We've been sold out for weeks."

Ethan slid his hand to Lizzy's waist. "Is there anything you can do for us?"

"I'm not sure. Let me check something really quick." The manager's fingers flew across the keyboard. He glanced at the screen and then back at Ethan and Lizzy. "Are you okay sitting in a different spot?"

There was hope for them, after all. Lizzy nodded. She didn't care where she was in the theater, as long as she could see the show.

The manager printed out new tickets and handed them over with a wink. "I think you guys are going to be happy. Enjoy the show."

Lizzy couldn't believe their luck. She took Ethan's hand and began to walk towards the back of the theater. The seats wouldn't be as good, but at least they were something. She was admiring the costumes on display when Ethan tugged her hand, pulling her in the opposite direction.

"That was where the old seats were," she said. "I'm sure all that's left are the back rows."

Ethan shook his head, a grin spreading across his face. "The manager wasn't kidding when he said we'd be happy." He held out the tickets.

Lizzy read the seat numbers, blinking a few times to

make sure she was seeing the right thing. "We're in the front row."

Lizzy's heart pounding with each number. She had never been so close to the stage before. Each dancer twirled by with grace, their skirts billowing around their legs. Singers walked down the aisles, passing close enough for Lizzy to reach out and touch them.

By the time intermission came along, she felt like she was floating. "This is absolutely incredible." She kissed Ethan's cheek. "Thank you for an amazing evening. I don't want it to end."

Ethan smoothed down her hair. "I've heard the second half is even better."

The curtain went up for the second act, and Lizzy watched the stage, waiting for the first of the performers to appear. Instead, a man dressed in a tuxedo walked slowly onto the stage, a microphone in his hand.

"We'd like to thank everyone for coming tonight. A few years ago, we started a tradition that I think you'll enjoy. Please join us in learning a few steps of our next dance. If you're able to, you can stand and follow along from your seats."

The music began to play, and a row of dancers walked onto the stage. Lizzy laughed as she tried to follow the steps. Chuckles filled the audience as the dancers began to move faster and faster. Their moves were impossible to follow.

After a pause, the man held up the microphone again.

"That was pretty good, but I think we need a little more help. Can I have a few volunteers from the audience?"

Lizzy didn't register that the movement by her side was Ethan, holding his hand high in the air. "Put that down," she said, bumping his side with her hip. She rubbed a hand across her forehead. "I was awful at that dance."

Ethan looked at her face, his eyebrows raised. "Me too. It's all part of the adventure, though. Right?"

"True." Lizzy held his gaze while she raised her hand.

A pair of dancers dressed in jingling shoes ran through the audience, choosing people at random. Lizzy began to breathe easier when the elves ran onto the stage, followed by the volunteers. The man with the microphone invited everyone to sit down.

Now, the show kicked up a notch. Each volunteer was paired up with a dancer, and together, they lifted their feet to practice the moves everyone had just learned. Without warning, another pair of dancers ran onto the stage, brushing down their costumes while they tried to blend into the group.

"Stop!" The man with the microphone glared at the latecomers, earning a giggle from the audience. He turned to face them. "It appears that someone forgot to come on time. We need one more couple." He glanced down at the audience, pointing straight at Lizzy and Ethan.

"You two will do. Up you get."

Before Lizzy could react, hands were pulling her onto the stage. There wasn't time to say anything before Ethan was swept away to join his partner. The music turned back on, and everyone began dancing. Lizzy followed along with her partner, stopping when he stopped and moving forward when he pulled her along. After a moment, the music came to a crescendo.

"It's time for the finale," her partner whispered. "We're going to pass you down the line until you end up back with your handsome gentleman friend. Ready?"

Lizzy nodded. She let the music take her away, smiling while hands spun her from one person to the next. Before she knew it, she was standing in front of Ethan, who sank to the ground on bended knee, holding his hands out.

Electricity poured out of his eyes when he grabbed her hands. Lizzy gave them a gentle tug to help him stand up, but he didn't move. It took her a moment to realize that the man with the microphone was standing next to Ethan.

Her heart began to skip when Ethan reached for the microphone. "Lizzy Thompson. Some people know, from the moment they meet, that they are destined to be together. I can't say the same about us."

That earned a low chuckle from the audience, but Lizzy's pulse was pounding too loudly in her ears to pay them any attention.

"I never imagined that the fiery woman who challenged me every step would become someone I couldn't live without. We may not have started as friends, but I can't imagine my life now without you in it. You make me a better man. I know life will always have challenges to navigate. We aren't going to agree on everything that happens, but I want to spend every day of the rest of my life working it out with you."

He reached into his pocket and pulled out a small box which he flipped open. Nestled between two layers of silk was a diamond ring. Lizzy's heart was ready to burst.

"You are my best friend, and I love you more and more every day. Will you marry me?"

Lizzy couldn't speak. She nodded her head enthusiastically before finding her words. "Yes, yes. A million times, yes."

The audience roared when Lizzy bent over to kiss Ethan, pulling him to his feet.

Ethan's hands were shaking when he slid the ring onto her finger where it would stay, conceivably, for the rest of forever.

* * *

Hours later, Lizzy snuggled on the couch next to Ethan's side. Her hand felt heavy now, with a ring that held promise. She held her hand out in front of her, turning it from side to side so she could admire the diamond.

"How did you know which style I'd like best?"

Ethan rested his chin on her head. "I may have had a little help from Maisy. Did we get it right?"

"It is perfect. I can't believe you were able to pull that off." She knew she'd remember their impromptu dance for the rest of her life. "How did you get the theater to cooperate?"

"That part was easy. I've been giving the cast members free cookies after every show. They love me over there."

Lizzy watched the diamond cast sparkles onto the couch beside her. "Thank you for making the night so special. I loved it, and I love you."

There were hundreds of details they would have to figure out, but for now, Lizzy was content to sit by Ethan's side. She lifted her chin to his, kissing him softly. "I can't wait for forever to begin."

* * *

Thanks for reading Lizzy and Ethan's story. If you'd like to keep up with my latest projects, visit ruthpendleton.com.

Made in the USA
Columbia, SC
23 April 2024